Praise for *We Can* also by Cat

‘Remarkable. Witty, wise and compelling’ *Sunday Times*

‘Deserves high praise. Thoughtful and well-written’
Evening Standard

‘Astonishing, inventive . . . A remarkable piece of work’
Books for Keeps

‘This is a book with high ambitions – it tries to do many things and pulls them all off – tender, sad, but also tense and exciting. An excellent read’ Anthony McGowan

‘The kind of writing that appeals to both kids and adults, in the same way as Mark Haddon and Michael Morpurgo’
Financial Times

‘Outstanding . . . A big, brave debut’ *The Bookseller*

‘Wonderful’ *Thirst for Fiction*

‘An astonishing debut’ *Lovereading*

‘Sensitive and explosive’ *Inis*

‘Funny and very realistic’
Sally Nicholls, author of *Ways to Live Forever*

‘I can’t imagine a single reader who wouldn’t love this book. Bruton’s dialogue truly sparkles’ *Bookbag*

‘Hugely entertaining. Perfect for fans of Michael Morpurgo and Frank Cottrell Boyce’ Red House Books

Books by Catherine Bruton

We Can be Heroes

Pop!

I Predict a Riot

After graduating from the University of Oxford, Catherine Bruton began her career as an English teacher and later went on to write feature articles for *The Times* and other publications. *I Predict a Riot* is her third novel for Egmont, following *We Can Be Heroes* and *Pop!*, which received high acclaim. Catherine lives near Bath with her husband and two children.

I PREDICT A RIOT

CATHERINE BRUTON

First published in Great Britain 2014
by Electric Monkey, an imprint of Egmont UK Limited
The Yellow Building, 1 Nicholas Road, London W11 4AN

ISBN 978 1 4052 6719 9

1 3 5 7 9 10 8 6 4 2

www.egmont.co.uk

A CIP catalogue record for this title is available from the British Library

Typeset by Avon DataSet Ltd, Bidford on Avon, Warwickshire
Printed and bound in Great Britain by the CPI Group

55240/1

For all my Peckham people,
Clare, Howard, Nye, Nicola, James,
Jo, Millie, Jonny, Joe and Elsie the Twinkle,
with love.

SCENE 1: MAGGIE'S HOUSE, BY THE SEA

It's been a year since everything happened, but I still have bad dreams. Dreams of last summer – of me and Tokes and Little Pea – in the park, under the arches, racing through burning streets on the night the city was in flames. It's like a movie running through my head – the same one night after night. Then I wake up to the sound of the waves and I remember how the story ends.

We live by the sea now, my mum and me. In a house with a long garden that runs down to a pebbly beach, far away from where it all happened. I can see the water from my bedroom window, hear the waves lapping on the pebbles. And there's nothing to do here but remember how one of my friends is dead and the other one might as well be. All because of me.

I think he has a new name now which would make Little Pea laugh because he always reckoned it was a stupid name. He's got a whole new identity too: new home, new life – new start.

A witness-protection programme. The police had to make him and his whole family disappear so Shiv and the Starfish Gang would never find them. And that means they can't tell me where he is and I can never contact him. Ever. No phone, no text, no email, no Facebook. Nothing. It's for his own safety, I suppose, but he probably never wants to see or speak to me again anyway.

Most days I watch the film we made last summer. I've had a long time to try and finish it, but it still feels like something is missing. Even though I've cut and edited bits, changed angles, altered the soundtrack, I can't ever seem to change the story it tells. Just like in my dreams.

SCENE 2: A PARK IN SOUTH LONDON

'The boys are back in town!' Little Pea was singing.

All the other kids in the park had gone silent. Little Pea was perched on one of the kiddie swings like some kind of weird boy-bird, staring in the direction of the approaching Starfish Gang who were obviously going to beat him to a squishy pulp. But he kept on singing like a canary in a cage.

He knew what was coming. I'd zoomed in so the lens of my camera was staring right into his pupils. If you ask any film director, they'll tell you it's all in the eyes and, even though Little Pea had this massive crazy smile spread over his funny baby face as he sang, you could tell from his eyes that he knew he was in for a beating.

If this had been a proper film, it would be a gangster movie or maybe a Western. There'd be whistling wind in the background, or the strumming of a lone guitar as the baddies walked into view across the horizon while the little guy trembled and prayed for the hero to ride in and rescue him. Only there was no hero coming to rescue Little Pea from what I could see. Because real life isn't like the movies, is it? That's what my mum's always saying anyway.

I was perched in the middle of the roundabout, cross-legged, filming everything, but trying to pretend my camera was just a mobile phone so nobody would realise. I think I knew that if the Starfish Gang caught me they'd smash my camera – and probably me too. But I thought I was invisible in those days. Invisible and safe. I was wrong on both counts.

Little Pea was acting like he wasn't worried either. 'The boys are back! The boys are back!' he squawked, high-pitched, bird-like, kind of out of tune.

Little Pea was in Year 8 so I suppose that made him about twelve, but he looked no bigger than a nine-year-old. I'd heard someone say he was a fully-grown adult midget; and another who reckoned his mum had been poisoning him and stunted his growth. I'd even heard a rumour that he was an alien or that he'd been abducted by aliens who'd shrunk him on their spaceship! There were a lot of rumours about Little Pea.

Pea wasn't his real name either, but it kind of suited him because he had this small round face and eyes that looked kind of green in the light, although they were twinkling with what looked like fear now as he stared in the direction of the Starfish Gang.

With my camera perched on my knee, I could catch their shadows as they walked across the concrete, and the white clouds scudding across the high-rise flats behind them. It made them look like they were walking in slow motion. Or maybe that was something they did – another trick to make themselves seem even scarier. Like everyone in the neighbourhood wasn't scared enough of them already.

No one messed with the Starfish Gang. Even I knew that, and I wasn't even from around there. Not really. I knew about the drug raps, the robberies, the street wars and stabbings and shootings. And about the army of local kids they had running errands for them all over town. Rumour had it that Shiv, the gang leader, stabbed some kid over in North London, and that Tad, his number two, carried a gun shoved down his left sock.

How did I know? Because I watched and I listened. That's something all the great film directors do. I read it in an interview in a film magazine: you have to sit in cafes and bus stops and parks and listen to people, find stories. There are stories all around you, all the time, it said. Stories waiting to be told.

So that's what I used to do, ever since my mum and dad split up anyway. My mum said I needed to stop filming other people's lives and live my own, but she didn't get it. That was exactly *why* I did it: to escape into other people's stories so I didn't have to think about my own rubbish life at all.

*

That day the Starfish Gang strode across the park like they owned it, their jeans hanging so low you could see pretty much all of their boxer shorts, their baseball caps resting on the top of their heads like they were far too small. And at the front was Shiv, the gang leader, skinny like a snake with a face the colour of storm clouds, wearing this long black leather coat that flapped round his ankles. It made him look like a vampire.

He had marks on his cheeks, symmetrical half-moon scars, mirror images below the whites of his pale milky eyes. I think I'd heard someone say he was only seventeen, but his eyes glared like his insides were rotting away in his belly. It made you wonder what he'd seen to make him look that way. Or what he'd done.

He came to a stop about five metres short of the swings and the rest of the gang stopped behind him. Little Pea was still chirruping away. Shiv just stood there and stared at him – totally still, like you see lions doing on those wildlife programmes when they're about to pounce. There was a pause – it's just a couple of beats when you watch it back on film – before Pea stopped singing and fluttered down off the swing. He was grinning as if he was their puppy dog, but I caught a glimpse of his eyes and they were bright as buttons and blinking like mad.

'Whatcha, Shiv?' he chirped. He was doing a funny dance thing, like a cross between Riverdance and body-popping, and grinning nervously.

Shiv stayed silent. From the railway track that runs alongside the park came a distant ringing: that sound the rails make when a train is coming close.

'Whassup, Shiv-man?' Pea squeaked. 'What can I do for you, my main man, eh?' He was doing a moonwalk on the hot concrete now, in a pair of dirty white trainers with a Nike tick drawn on in pen.

'You, blud!' Shiv hissed. He took a step forward and Pea stopped dancing. 'You're whassup!'

'Why? What I done?' said Little Pea, mouth still grinning, but his eyes flicking from side to side.

'You know what you done,' Shiv said, taking another step forward. Pea darted backwards, tripping up over his feet. His fake trainers looked weirdly big for his tiny body.

'My cousin Pats got a beating cos of you, boy!' Shiv went on, tipping his head to one side and staring so hard at Pea he looked like he could pin him up against the fence just with his eyes.

'Hey, no way, Shiv-man!' Pea protested, wriggling backwards some more. 'I wasn't even there when it happen, bro!'

'*Ex-act-ly!*' said Shiv, spitting out each syllable. His eyes were thin black slits just like a snake, poised, ready to attack. 'You were s'posed to be on lookout, but the minute you see trouble you ghosted yourself away, innit?'

'No way,' said Pea, a high click of fear in his sing-song voice now. 'I did jus' what you tell me, Shiv-man.'

'Yeah?' Shiv's eyes widened just a fraction, the two black slits dark ovals for a moment. 'So why you do a runner when you seed the police comin', instead of soundin' the warnin'?'

Pea's face was flushed and there were little beads of sweat on his pinched cheeks. 'I never see dem comin', Shiv,' he squealed. 'They snuck up on me. I dittn't have no time to warn you!' His eyes were sparkling like Christmas lights and it was impossible to tell if he was lying or not.

'Not much of a lookout who don't see nuttin', eh?' Shiv snarled, taking another step forward, a swaying movement in his long black coat.

Behind him the rest of the Starfish Gang were lounging up against the swings, watching. Shiv's right-hand man, Tad, was standing on the kiddie swing, rocking gently. 'You need glasses?' he called out to Little Pea. 'Or mebbe you was too busy savin' you own self to bother lookin' out for nobody else?'

Pea stuttered out a few squeaky vowels, like a car engine that wouldn't start, then spluttered into silence. Shiv was up so close to him now they were almost touching. The sound of the approaching train wailed louder on the tracks, an insistent whine cutting through the searing heat of the day.

Shiv glanced around quickly. Looking for something? Checking the coast was clear? And, as his eyes swung over the roundabout, he clocked me sitting there and his eyes narrowed. Quick as a flash, I pretended I was texting on my 'phone'. Shiv stared at me for a moment before scanning over towards the gate.

I let out a sigh of relief and I probably should have just stopped filming then and disappeared, but I didn't. I guess I knew I wasn't really invisible, but I think I still thought I was safe. My mum was always going on about parallel universes. She said London was full of them, all existing side by side, but never really noticing each other. The Starfish Gang and Shiv and Little Pea belonged to one universe and I belonged to another and I thought that meant they couldn't touch me.

Shiv's snake eyes swung back to Little Pea.

'I stayed right where you told me, Shiv, I swear!' Little Pea yabbered on. His big fake Nikes jigged up and down on the ground as he spoke. He couldn't seem to keep still. 'Mebbe my eyes is goin' cack. Mebbe I needs to take myself down the op-ti-cian, but I promise I don't see nuttin'. I dittn't see da feds comin'.'

'You see who give my cousin Pats a beatin' then?' Shiv hissed.

'No, Shiv. He was fine when I see him.'

'Cos someone hurt him bad,' said Shiv, eyes boring into Pea

like he was the one who'd done it. 'Someone put him in hospital and they gonna pay for it, unnerstand?'

'Yeah, I unnerstand,' Pea said, head nodding frantically like those toy dogs you sometimes see in car windows.

'So, if you saw who done it, you bes' tell me, right?' Shiv glowered at Pea and, out of the blue, I remembered another thing I'd heard about him: that he'd smacked his own mum once, so hard he broke her jaw. I didn't know for definite if that was true – there were as many rumours about Shiv as there were about Pea – but looking at him then it was easy to believe.

Suddenly Shiv's hand was in his pocket and then in one swift movement it was up close to Little Pea's face. Little Pea squirmed and wriggled like a fish in a net and for a second I couldn't make out what was going on. And then I saw the narrow blade in Shiv's hand, pressed up against Pea's cheek, gleaming against the scars that ran over it.

If you watch the film, you can hear me gasp when that happens. Shiv might be named after the knife people say he cut the scars on his own face with, but I was still shocked when he pulled it out. And that was when we had the proper 'movie magic' moment. The little blade caught the light and sent a disc of fire flashing into my camera lens, obscuring everything in a haze of white. Then, as the viewfinder cleared, I caught sight of the New Kid.

I'd never seen him before, but I knew right away he wasn't from Coronation Road. Not because he looked different exactly. It was just the way he kept walking, like he hadn't noticed anything was up. Like he didn't have a clue who the Starfish Gang were. He was walking right into the middle of a war zone and didn't seem to realise it.

There was a perfect backdrop to the scene. The grass behind him was yellow and sparse, and beyond that there was a view over the whole of Coronation Road, over the terraces and shops and the miles of tower blocks towards the city in the distance. You could even see the giant wheel of the London Eye nestled between the skyscrapers and the white clouds. And the New Kid had the sun shining on him as he walked towards us, just like the hero in a cowboy movie.

Shiv hadn't spotted him yet and neither had the rest of the Starfish boys, but Little Pea had, and his eyes widened in surprise. The New Kid was only about ten metres away, but he had on a massive pair of headphones and seemed lost in his own world. He had a face like chocolate sunshine, I thought. I wanted to call out to stop him, but something made me hesitate.

'You gonna ansa me or what?' Shiv hissed. The blade was tight against Little Pea's neck. 'You gonna tell me who put my cousin Pats in hospital or am I gonna do da same for you?'

'Um . . .' said Pea, looking desperately around him like somebody might be able to give him the right answer. Like he could phone a friend or click his heels together and go up in a puff of smoke. He glanced at me and at a couple of little kids who were playing over in the mucky sandpit.

The sun was shining directly on Pea so the mass of tiny scars on his cheeks, similar to Shiv's, stood out clearly like chicken-pox craters only more symmetrical. Even his scalp, beneath his closely shaved head, was criss-crossed with pale scar lines, like someone had drawn them on with something sharp, or splattered hot wax all over him.

The train was close by, its screech staining the air with noise. And I knew deep in my stomach that it wasn't right to be filming this. That standing by and letting it happen was wrong. But that was when I realised that the New Kid had stopped and was staring. Shiv and the Starfish boys still hadn't clocked him, but he'd seen them and he had this look on his face – not scared, but sort of angry, and also something else I couldn't make out.

Little Pea started to giggle, a hiccupy, high-pitched giggle, as the train came hurtling along the track. And suddenly Shiv grabbed him and pushed him up against the railings so his massive feet were dangling just above the ground and he was choking, spluttering, coughing. He cried out and I saw a thin trickle of red run down his neck and drop on to his trainers.

Then the New Kid was right behind Shiv, pulling him off Pea. The train was still going past, roaring behind their heads. And I definitely should have stopped filming then. If I had then maybe things wouldn't have gone like they did. But I kept the camera rolling as the New Kid grabbed Shiv by the collar and pushed him up against the railings while Pea fell to the ground and slithered out of the way, like a small animal. I was frightened suddenly; my heart was racing so hard I swear you can hear it on the film.

The New Kid looked younger than Shiv – my sort of age, fourteen, fifteen maybe – and smaller too, with cocoa-brown skin, eyes like pebbles and an open face that could not have been more different to the sly, bolting, mad look on Shiv's. Shiv was panting fast; the New Kid had taken him by surprise. And he might have been smaller than Shiv, but he was strong, because Shiv couldn't seem to push him off. But the weirdest thing was that he didn't look frightened at all; he just looked gutted, totally gutted, and I remember thinking: heroes aren't supposed to look like that, are they? Not when they're riding in to save the day.

There was a pause – 4.6 seconds it lasts on the film loop. Shiv stopped struggling and just glared down at the New Kid who stared right back at him, and neither of them said a word. No one else dared say anything either. Tad and the rest of the Starfish Gang were a few metres behind the New Kid, standing in a line, fists balled, unmoving. Pea was still sprawled out on the ground, watching. Nobody moved a muscle. I guess nobody had ever seen anyone get the better of Shiv before and we were all waiting to see what would happen next.

After 4.7 seconds, the New Kid let go so fast that Shiv's knees buckled. Then the New Kid shrugged his shoulders and started walking away. I think he said something, but you can't make it out on the film because there was a siren wailing in the background. Shiv caught it though. His face flashed with a spasm of anger and for a second it looked as if he was going to lunge at the New Kid. He didn't. He just pulled himself upright and stared, like he could stab him with his eyes.

'Come on.' The New Kid was offering a hand to Pea, who was still sprawled on the floor among the broken glass and the empty crisp packets and old tin cans.

But Little Pea looked up at him and gave him this weird grin. He glanced at Shiv then back at the New Kid's outstretched hand. Then he shook his head and giggled in his strange, tinny way. 'No way, crazy boy!'

The New Kid sighed, like he hadn't expected Pea to take his hand anyway. 'Suit yourself,' he said with a shrug.

Shiv started to laugh. His pale eyes were glinting and his laughter was hard and angry. 'Hey, come on, Little Pea,' he crooned. 'Come to mamma!'

In the movies the little guy never goes running back to the

villain. Not after the hero has rescued him from mortal peril. But Little Pea seemed to have forgotten that Shiv had been about to stick him with a knife two minutes before. He just jumped up and trotted over obediently. Shiv stood up and brushed down his long leather coat, staring the whole time at the New Kid, who stared right back.

The rest of the Starfish Gang were still lined up a few metres away. Tad looked like a dog straining on a leash, waiting for a nod from Shiv to tell him to rip the New Kid's throat out.

And Pea? He was jiggling on the spot like he needed a wee, and that was when he glanced in my direction and noticed my camera. I quickly pretended to send a text again, but not before I saw his beady eyes widen, just a fraction. Then he looked me right in the eye and grinned. And I could tell he knew.

The New Kid was pulling his earphones back on to his head and walking backwards in the direction of the park gates, his eyes all the time on Shiv.

From over by the swings Tad grunted, 'You gonna jus' let him walk away, Shiv? You gonna let him disrespec' you like that and walk outta here with his head still on his shoulders?' He was pumped up, ready for a fight, although his luminous white skin and pale eyelashes made him look a bit like a ghost.

But Shiv just stood there, watching the New Kid until he reached the gate. Then he called after him. 'Bes' watch your back from now on, boy!'

When you watch that bit of film you can tell – just like everyone in the park could tell – that the New Kid was dead meat. A marked man. Kaboom.

SCENE 3: CORONATION ROAD LIBRARY

I've always loved films. I love the stories and the music, but most of all I love the pictures: the close-ups, the long panoramic shots, the follow shots, even the blurry hand-held ones. I love the way the pictures tell the story, more than the words themselves. Me and words don't always get on very well. Like me and real life.

My dad got me a little digital video camera just before he and my mum split up. I think he knew he was going to leave; maybe that's why he bought it. Anyway, it was the best present ever. It was tiny – looked a bit like a smartphone and fitted into my pocket – but I could make proper movies with it. I don't think I went out anywhere without it since the day he gave it to me. He said I'd be the next Spielberg. My mum said it was just another thing for me to hide behind. I think they had a row about that as well. Two weeks later he left.

That's when I started filming everything. It felt like my life had fallen to pieces, so I started watching the world second hand through the lens instead. I filmed meals, train journeys, my feet on the pavement, the leaves in the garden. I even filmed the TV while I was watching it. I stopped looking directly at anything. And it made life so much less sharp, less painful. And more beautiful.

At school it meant I didn't have to talk to anyone. There's not much to make a film about at boarding school so mainly it kept me safe, cut off. But in the holidays, when I came back to London, my mum worked all the time and my dad had moved to New York so there was nothing for me to do but make movies.

I saw the New Kid the next day, down at the library. He was in the teenage books section, curled up on one of the big armchairs with a pile of books a mile high stacked up next to him. I could see one of the librarians giving him a funny look, like he shouldn't be there, like he didn't belong. But he was so deeply engrossed in what he was reading he didn't even notice.

It was funny, running into him like that – the sort of thing that normally only happens in the movies – especially since I realised I'd been hoping I'd see him again, the hero kid with the death wish.

I watched him for a bit, and it made me smile. He looked

like he was miles away in his head, like he'd totally forgotten real life even existed. I don't get that with books. Films, yes, but I'm dyslexic so words on a page jump around and won't stick in my head.

The New Kid didn't even notice when a group of mums and toddlers started gathering for a storytelling session nearby, until the librarian lady went over and asked him to move. Then he looked up like he'd just resurfaced from a deep-sea dive. His brown eyes were like wet, faraway pebbles.

'Oh, yeah, right,' he said. 'Sorry.' He scrambled up, gathered his books and made his way over to the front desk.

So I followed him. I didn't film him, but I just sort of hung out nearby while he tried to check out his books.

'I'm sorry, but if you want to register for the library you need to bring your parent or guardian with you,' the lady behind the desk was saying in a posh, crinkly voice that didn't really fit with the way she looked – lumpy cardigan, hair the colour of mildew, tired eyes.

'But my mum works,' the New Kid was saying. 'She works, like, all the time.'

'Your father then?'

The New Kid frowned when she said this. His pebble eyes went blank and I wished I'd been filming then so I could catch his expression.

'No worries,' he said, putting the books down on the desk

and pulling his massive earphones back on to his head. 'I'll just leave it.'

He went out into the lobby then and called the lift. I kept following him, because he had somehow become the hero of my film and I needed to see how his story panned out.

The lift doors hovered open and I jumped in just before they closed. I stared at the New Kid's feet, and his hands which seemed empty without a book in them.

'Are you following me?'

I jumped. He was looking at me and I felt myself go bright red. The lift was probably halfway down. 'No,' I murmured.

He tugged his earphones off and looked at me even harder than before.

'I saw you in the park yesterday, didn't I?' he said. 'When it all kicked off. You were there.'

I could feel myself going pinker by the minute. I gave a sort of shrug.

The lift doors opened. We both hesitated, then the New Kid stepped back to let me go out first, like my dad always does. Did.

'Thanks,' I said quietly, avoiding his eye as we both stepped out into the lobby and headed towards the exit.

'Seriously, are you some kind of spy or what?' said the New Kid, when we reached the glass doors. He had a look in his eyes that might have been a challenge or might have been amusement.

'Don't be silly,' I said. The words came out way posher sounding than I meant them to.

The New Kid gave me another weird look then turned round and shrugged as he stepped out on to the concrete outside.

Coronation Road Library is an award-winning design, my dad told me once. It's built in the shape of a C – for Coronation Road – and it's all multicoloured glass and chrome. Outside, in the curve of the C, is a courtyard scattered with these giant stone globes, some half submerged in the concrete, some barely rising out of the surface, and all covered in tiny multicoloured tiles. There are some strange metal benches that look more like sculptures than seats, and they're dead uncomfortable. Some people hate that library – my mum included – but my dad and I like the shapes, the way they intersect with the sky and the rubble and the estate that runs for miles behind them.

The New Kid plonked himself down on one of the funny sculpture benches. 'You want to join me?' he asked, looking up and staring me right in the eye.

I hesitated for a second before I said, 'Um, OK.'

So I perched next to him and we sat there, watching the pigeons and not saying much. He definitely wasn't your typical hero, this skinny, smiley-faced bookworm, who went around saving kids from being stabbed in the park. But there was something about him, some kind of quality which seemed to shine out of him, even here, surrounded by litter and concrete.

'Why did you do it?' I asked.

'Do what?' said the New Kid.

I bit my lip nervously. 'Um, help Little Pea in the park yesterday.'

'Is Little Pea the boy with the big shoes?'

I nodded and waited for him to go on, but he didn't, so I said, 'So why did you then? Do it?'

He shrugged and looked up at the cloudless blue sky. It had been one of the hottest summers on record. There had been no rain for so many weeks that everyone had forgotten what a cloudy sky looked like. 'Probably cos I'm an idiot,' he said.

'I thought you were brave,' I said, feeling my cheeks burning again. 'I never saw anyone stand up to the Starfish Gang before.'

'Maybe. It was still stupid,' he said. Then he sighed. 'I promised my mum two things: to stay out of trouble and always brush my teeth.' He turned to me with a grin that didn't reach his eyes. 'And what do I go and do? Get myself in a whole heap of trouble first week of the school holidays.'

I wanted to ask him why his mum made him promise to stay out of trouble, but I didn't want him to think I was prying into his business, so I just said, 'Your teeth look OK.'

He grinned with his big sunshine smile, properly this time, and I found myself smiling back.

'Who did you say those other kids were anyway?' he asked. 'The ones who were beating on Pea or whatever you say his name is?'

'The Starfish Gang?' I said, staring down at my thin, grubby fingers. 'And the boy with the knife is called Shiv. Shiv Karunga.'

The New Kid looked down at the tatty Vans on his feet and frowned.

'You're not from around here, are you?' I said.

A shadow passed over his eyes and he said quickly, 'It's none of your business where I'm from.'

'Sorry,' I said quietly.

He sighed again. 'No, I'm sorry. I don't mean to bite your head off. It's just . . .' He hesitated, then said something I wasn't expecting. 'You filmed it all, right?'

My fingers curled tightly round the camera in my pocket.

'I saw you with a camera so I figured maybe you filmed what happened.'

He was looking me up and down and I wondered what I looked like to him: a skinny, purple-haired girl with a face like a freckly elf, wearing an ET T-shirt, boys' surfing shorts and massive cherry-red boots.

He had the kind of face you couldn't lie to, so I just nodded.

'You got it with you then?'

I pulled my camera out of my pocket and passed it to him, looking down at my hands again.

'Cool,' he said, checking it out. He flicked it on and pressed the play button. The footage I'd taken in the park yesterday appeared on the tiny screen and his own face came into view – close up, with that gutted-and-something-else expression I couldn't make out.

His brow furrowed as he watched, but he didn't say anything. He let it play for another thirty seconds or so then turned it off.

'Yup, I'm an idiot!' he said, handing it back to me. 'So do you always go around filming people when they're not looking?'

'I didn't exactly mean to,' I said awkwardly. 'I'm sort of making a movie.'

'Serious?' He looked genuinely interested.

'There's this competition,' I found myself saying, 'for young film-makers, and I want to enter it.'

I shrugged and looked down at my beloved cherry-red, steel-cap DM boots, with a sad face Tippexed on one foot and a happy face on the other. My mum hated those boots so I wore them every single day, even when it was blisteringly hot and my feet were totally boiling like they were that day.

I think I'd have worn them in bed if I could.

'What's it about?' he asked. 'Your film.'

'I'm not exactly sure yet,' I said. My face felt as red as my boots. 'I don't really have a story. I just film stuff.'

'What sort of stuff?'

My toes wiggled uncomfortably. 'Just stuff around here. The Coronation Road, the Starfish Estate. Inner-city kids living in parallel universes. That kind of thing.'

'Right,' he said, looking at me curiously for a second. 'Um – why?'

I scrunched up my toes some more. If I told him the whole story, I'd have to tell him about my mum, and about dad leaving and everything. So I just said, 'I don't know really. It's just what there is around here.'

He grinned again unexpectedly. I figured if anyone'd been filming us right then we'd have looked an odd couple. Then he said something else I wasn't expecting. 'I could help, you know?'

I tried not to look as freaked out as I felt when I said, 'Really?' But I don't think I exactly managed it.

'Yeah. I like stories. Words, you know? Maybe I could help with that bit.'

'Right,' I said, chewing my lip some more.

'And my mum said to keep out of trouble,' he went on. 'So maybe I can help you keep out of trouble too? Cos, you know, it's really not a good idea to go around filming guys like Shiv.' His eyes clouded a little as he said the last bit.

The Tippex faces on the toes of my boots seemed to wink up at me. 'My dad reckons filming keeps me out of mischief,' I said.

And I remembered the 'chat' we had on the day he walked out. 'Keep filming. Keep out of mischief. Look after your mother for me,' he'd said, like he was just going away on holiday, not leaving us for good. Then he'd given me one of his big hugs and walked out of the door.

'Yeah?' the New Kid said, giving me a funny look like he was trying to read the thoughts in my head. 'Well, maybe we can do it together. Look out for each other, you know? And make a movie at the same time.'

I looked really hard at him, disbelieving suddenly. Why did someone like him want to hang out with me? 'Seriously?'

'Sure,' he said. 'You do the pictures, I do the words and we both do the film-star bit!'

I smiled and twisted my fingers tightly round the camera. The sun was shining on the New Kid's face, making his chocolate skin glow and his Afro hair look like a halo round his head.

'So what's your name, director girl?' he asked.

'Maggie,' I said. Then I added quickly, 'Only that's not my real name.'

He raised his eyebrows. 'OK . . . um, what's your real name then?'

'Emmeline Margaret,' I said quickly. 'My mum thought I might be the pioneering type. You know, like Margaret Thatcher or Emmeline Pankhurst, the suffragette lady. Only nobody's ever called me that. They just call me Maggie.'

'Right. Well, Maggie's a good name. Suits you.'

'Thanks,' I nodded.

'I'm Tokes,' he said. 'Just Tokes.'

And then the New Kid – who was called Tokes, just Tokes – smiled. And I think maybe that's when we first became friends.

SCENE 4: OUTSIDE THE LIBRARY

'You are so dead!'

We both turned round and there was Little Pea, scrambling out from behind a load of wheelie bins and skipping towards us across the concrete. He had a brand-new black eye, but he was grinning widely. When he reached us, he did a little ballet hop then jumped to a standstill in front of our bench.

'Seriously, you pair is already in body bags, innit!' he squeaked with a flick of his head like he was performing a girl-band dance routine.

'Right,' said Tokes as Pea jiggled on the spot in front of us. 'And there's me thinking you'd come to thank me for saving your skin yesterday! How did you even find us?'

Pea giggled and flicked his head again, but didn't answer Tokes's question. 'Like I'm gonna thank you for jumpin' off a cliff an' takin' me wit' you,' he said, talking in his too-loud, too-fast, little-kid voice.

I looked at his black eye and wondered if any of the things I'd heard about him were true – the stuff about the jungle magic and juju and his mum trying to beat the devil out of him in church.

'Your girlfrien' tell you who you mess wit' yesterday, man?' Pea was saying, nodding and winking in my direction.

'She's not my girlfriend,' said Tokes, shooting me a quick look.

'If you say so!' Little Pea just winked at me again and said, 'Anyways, she probably already tell you that you nearly got me killed wit' your meddlin'.'

'Way I remember it, I rescued you from Shiv,' said Tokes. He spoke differently when he was talking to Pea. He sounded more, I dunno, like a kid from the streets rather than a guy who read piles of books in a library.

'I had it all under control!' said Pea breezily.

'Sure you did, kid,' said Tokes.

'Hey! Who you callin' kid?' Pea was still grinning like a maniac, and pretending to punch the air like a boxer. He seemed to be totally enjoying this. 'Don't you know to judge a man by his shoe size, an' these takkies tell you I twelve years old, man. Nearly a teenager me, innit.'

Tokes raised an eyebrow in surprise as Pea waggled his fake Nikes in the air, but he said nothing.

'How old is you anyway, alien boy?' demanded Little Pea.

'I'm fifteen,' said Tokes. 'And I'm no alien.'

'Well, you like an alien in this hood, bruv!' said Pea. 'Anyone can see that. An' you gonna get yourself killed too if you keep takin' on da locals. Which hood you from anyway?'

'None of your business,' said Tokes quickly. Too quickly, just like he'd jumped down my throat earlier when I'd asked the same question.

'Hey, don't go chewin' my head off, space boy!'

'Tokes,' I said quietly.

'You what?' said Pea, turning to me again with a funny little head movement. Honestly, I'd never seen a kid as fidgety as he was. Like a toddler, or a dog with fleas. 'You say summat, posh girl?'

'His name is Tokes,' I said. 'And I'm Maggie.'

Little Pea gave us each a look then folded up with giggles. His laugh was high-pitched, like a little girl's. 'An' I'm Little Pea, es-quire, at your ser-vice,' he said with a low bow, followed by a bit of a moonwalk. 'What kind of stupid name is Tokes anyway?'

'No more stupid than Little Pea!' Tokes retorted.

'Hey! Pea is short for Paris!' Pea went on. 'My mamma, she wanted to name me after Michael Jackson's kid. Only she got da girl's name by mistake.'

'Really?' I said.

'You think I gonna lie to you 'bout my own name?' he said,

with a hint of a challenge in his voice. 'It ain't every twelve-year-old midget can carry off a girl's name an' still stay mega-dope cool like me! Be-lieve!'

'Pea's good,' said Tokes with a shrug. 'It's . . . enigmatic.'

For some reason the long word didn't sound odd coming out of his mouth. He made it sound like a jewel, multicoloured and shiny and perfect. But Pea was looking at him suspiciously. I guessed not many people used big words around Pea. Or said nice things to him for that matter.

'You swallow a dictionary or summat?' he said.

'He likes books,' I said quietly.

'Oh yeah!' said Pea, his face lighting up like a Christmas tree suddenly. 'An' you like movies, innit.'

'What?' I said, flushing hotly.

'Yeah, I see you, all lights, camera, action! in da park yesterday!' Pea lurched back into another moonwalk with a massive grin. 'Hey! How cool was Shiv's face when Mr T-bone here had him against da wall?'

'I don't know what you're talking about.'

'You think nobody clocked your little filmin' stunt?' said Little Pea. 'Cos these eyes see everyt'ing, I tell you! Figure you don't want me to tell Shiv 'bout it, am I right?'

'No, she doesn't,' said Tokes.

'Cos you know you gonna get yourself a ticket to da morgue if you keep filmin' da Starfish boys, right?' said Pea, looking straight at me with his eyes that flickered and danced as much as his crazy feet.

'That's what I told her,' said Tokes quietly.

'If Shiv find out you got footage of da T-man disrespectin' him, he ain't gonna be best pleased. Mr Shiv value his hard-man rep-u-ta-tion! An' you, boy, you already got a price on your head for dissin' da Shiv-man on his turf,' said Pea, grinning at Tokes like he'd forgotten it was all his fault Tokes was in trouble in the first place. 'So, if Shiv find out 'bout Spielberg's little film, she good as dead, innit.'

'Nobody better tell him then, had they?' said Tokes.

'Ex-act-ly!' whispered Little Pea loudly. 'Bes' keep it on the down-low. All hush-hush an' that, right?'

'Right,' said Tokes. He gave Little Pea a look, and Pea met it with a grin that didn't promise anything.

'Hey! I real good at keepin' secrets!' Pea insisted. 'You see me in da park – even when I got a knife in my face I don't spill.'

'Spill what?' I said.

'Wouldn't you like to know!' said Pea, with a shimmying shrug. 'If I got intel, I ain't gonna reveal till it worth my while. That's all I'm sayin'.'

'So what's it gonna take for you to keep quiet about this then?' said Tokes.

Pea ignored him and turned to me. 'Way I see it, you

wanna buy my silence you gonna have to let me star in your film, innit.'

Tokes looked at him suspiciously. 'How do you even know she's making a film?'

'Ain't nuttin' happen in Coronation Road wi'out Little Pea got his eyes on it,' Little Pea said, his face gleaming.

'So you were spying on us? Listening into our conversation?'

'I can't reveal my sources!' said Pea with a big grin.

Tokes shook his head and Little Pea went on excitedly, 'But I wanna be one of them reality TV stars. *Only Way is the Starfish, Made in Coronation Road* – that sorta thing!' He looked at me and I couldn't help thinking that people would totally want to watch him. It was hard to take your eyes off his weird twitchy body and his crazy, mad-as-the-moon little baby face.

'Seriously?' Tokes said. 'That's what you want in return? To be in our movie?'

'Da Pea wants what it wants.' Pea shrugged. 'I got a good backstory too.' He kept glancing at me, grinning like we had some kind of secret between us. 'I 'spect you heard that I'm possessed by da devil, right?'

Tokes raised his eyebrows.

'She knows, innit,' Pea said, turning to me. 'Everyone round here knows I got da devil man in me bones. I got da scars to prove it too.' He lifted up his top to show his torso. It was etched with more of the tiny scars he had on his face, as well as round red patches. I imagined tracing the indentations with the camera, focusing in on the raised white scar tissue.

'Who did that to you?' Tokes demanded.

'Like I say, I only reveal intel when I ready!' Pea quickly tugged down his top with a sly grin. 'But I got other stuff for your film too,' he said. 'You know anyt'ing 'bout gangs, alien boy?'

Tokes's brow furrowed. 'Yes,' he said quietly, his eyes suddenly unreadable again. 'I know about gangs.'

'Well, there gonna be gang war in Coronation Road real soon,' Pea said with a manic grin. 'You hear 'bout Shiv's cousin Pats, yeah? He got seriously mashed yesterday, an' now he in hospital with a cracked skull an' punctured lung. Shiv say they gonna stick da villain what done it,' Pea went on. 'Or shoot his fool head off. An' they not kiddin' neither. Tad got him a shooter – I seen it.'

'Right,' said Tokes, his eyes faraway again like he was remembering something.

'And I know who did it!' Pea announced triumphantly.

'So you *did* see it happen?' I said.

Pea glanced around him, like he was playing spies or something, then he whispered loudly, 'I tell you – Da Pea see everyt'ing!'

'So why didn't you tell Shiv?' said Tokes. 'He had a knife against your throat.'

'I had it all unner control!' said Pea. 'Until you come along and nearly got me killed. I was gonna tell Shiv who hurt his cuz when the time was right, innit.'

Tokes shook his head in disbelief. 'So did you?' he asked. 'After we left, did you tell him what you saw?'

'I mighta dropped a few hints!' Pea giggled. 'Either way, it not gonna stay secret long. Not around here. Then it all gonna kick off like you would not believe. An' then you gonna have a well good story for that film of yours, I'm a-tellin' you.'

I glanced at Tokes who just rolled his eyes.

'Why?' I said.

Pea smirked and his eyes twinkled like he had the most delicious and dangerous secret in the world.

'All I gonna say is this is so much bigger than anyt'ing what ever happen in Coronation Road.'

'What's that got to do with her film?' Tokes asked.

I glanced at him. His eyes had the troubled look I'd seen in the park.

'Cos it gonna be movie gold, man!' said Pea. 'You win an Oscar filmin' this. It gonna be da war to end all wars.'

Tokes sighed. 'I'm supposed to be staying out of trouble,' he said.

'Well, mebbe you shoulda thought of that before you take on Shiv in da park, man,' said Pea with another giggle. 'But since you was tryin' to help out Da Pea – stop me from turnin' into a mushy pea – I'm givin' you a tip-off. An' cos you new round here and I kinda like you, even though you a crazy fool.'

Tokes rolled his eyes. 'Right,' he said. 'Look, I've gotta go.' He turned to me with a question in his eyes, like he was saying, 'You coming or what?'

'Mebbe I come wit' youse,' Pea cut in, his voice anxious suddenly, like a little kid who's desperate to be friends. 'Hangin' out wit' a pair of future corpses should be fun, innit.'

Tokes frowned again and I got the feeling that he didn't like this, but then he hesitated and glanced at the ground, as if he'd remembered something again.

'Sure,' he said reluctantly. 'Just don't go expecting me to rescue you next time.'

'You a funny man!' said Little Pea with a pleased grin spreading over his face. 'I can handle myself, innit. Don't need no one to rescue Little Pea.' He was defiantly hopping on one leg and flinging a few upper-cut punches into the air in front of him. 'I look out for myself – always have. Ain't no one gonna mess wit' me!'

'If you say so,' said Tokes.

'Come on then!' said Pea. 'Let's make a movie.' He grinned at me like we were best friends suddenly. 'An' mebbe, just mebbe, if you treat me nice, I tell you da biggest secret in Coronation Road.'

SCENE 5: CORONATION ROAD

So that's how the three of us ended up walking up Coronation Road on a boiling-hot day in August. Tokes went striding ahead like he was already regretting saying Pea could come, while Little Pea skipped along at my side.

'Nice hairdo,' he said, smirking. 'Same purple rinse as my granny!'

I felt the colour rising in my cheeks.

'Like the boots too,' he said. 'You do dem yourself?'

'Did you do your trainers yourself too?' I muttered, nodding down at his fake Nikes.

'Ooh, the white film chick got attitude!' he said, clicking his fingers excitedly.

I looked at him and he looked at me and he held my gaze, his eyes sparkling with mischief. Then he giggled. 'You know I got what it takes to be a film star, dontcha? Even if alien boy don't recognise my star quality yet.'

'Maybe,' I said.

Pea did a little hop like I'd just told him he'd won an Oscar. 'You jus' wait, gran'ma!'

Tokes turned round, caught my eye and then frowned at Little Pea. He looked worried, but he didn't say anything.

Coronation Road is the main artery running through that part of London and it's where all the parallel universes collide. There are Ghanaian groceries selling plantains and mealiepap and tiny smelly fish; Caribbean meat stalls with goats' heads on the wall and ox tongues on giant platters of ice, blood swilling out over the pavement. There are Asian silk shops and tiny Japanese booths selling every type of international calling card. There are pound shops and pawnbrokers; wig shops with windows full of rainbow-coloured hair extensions and skin-lightening creams; nail bars with jewel-encrusted talons – rows and rows of them, glimmering on display. And in among all these are the chain stores, struggling for air, not so high and mighty here. The only thing the shops have in common, my dad said, is that they all have the grumpiest, most unhelpful shop assistants you've ever come across in your life. We used to laugh about that all the time. My dad always used to be able to make me laugh – it's the thing I miss most since he's gone.

And anything can happen on Coronation Road. People deal drugs in broad daylight, sell knock-off videos, braid hair, cure toothache, piss, pray, break up, make up. I heard one couple got married there once, outside Fry-days Fish and Chip Bar, and that a baby was born on the floor of Beyoncé Hair and Beauty. I even heard that the Queen and her sister visited when they were little girls, and half the road got bombed to rubble in the Blitz. Basically, Coronation Road is like a film set with a million storylines and that's why I love it more than any other place on earth.

'So what you gonna call your film, huh?' Pea squeaked excitedly. 'I was thinkin' mebbe *Stars of the Starfish*? Whatcha think?'

'I don't really know yet,' I muttered.

'Me, I born an' bred on da Starfish Estate, innit,' Pea went on, nodding towards the square mile of tower blocks behind the library at the other end of Coronation Road. 'Cut me in half, you find "Starfish" written down da middle of me like a stick of rock. Not like Mr T here,' he chirped. 'He got another hood tattooed on his blood, I reckon.'

Tokes didn't turn round, but I could see the muscles in the back of his neck tensing.

'Chill out, man,' said Little Pea who seemed to be enjoying Tokes's unease. 'Jus' makin' small talk, innit.' Then he turned to me and winked. 'No need to tell me where you live, Hollywood, cos everyone know that.'

Tokes turned at that and walked backwards, like he felt he needed to keep an eye on Pea, like he didn't trust him not to stab him in the back. 'Why?' he demanded. 'How you know where she lives?'

Little Pea smirked and let out a loud laugh that was too big for his tiny body. 'No way!' I felt my cheeks hotter than ever as Pea's face lit up with a delighted grin. 'You tellin' me he don't even know 'bout your mamma?'

I glared at him, but I knew there was no point; he was bursting to tell and there was nothing I could do to stop him.

'She dittn't tell you her mamma is bessie mates with da Prime Minister?' Pea squeaked on, his tongue flicking in and out of his mouth.

Tokes was still looking at me, but I just stared down at my boots, wishing I could disappear into the cherry-red faces.

'She probably BFFs with Her Majesty da Queen too,' said Pea. 'Am I right?'

Tokes was still looking at me. 'Is he serious?'

'Sort of,' I muttered. 'She's an MP.'

'Dat mean Member of Par-lia-ment!' Pea announced.

'I know what it means,' said Tokes, giving him a look. Then he turned back to me and said, 'That's pretty cool.'

'It is so *not* cool!' I muttered quickly.

'She bit touchy 'bout it, I thinkin',' said Pea. 'Mebbe dat why she makin' a film 'bout how rubbish it is in her mamma's hood. It a party political broadcast to make her mamma look bad!'

'That's not what I'm doing!' I said, but I could feel my face flushing because he was right, in a way.

'If you say so, girlfrien'!' said Pea with a jerky hand gesture. 'Don't take a spy to figure out you an' your mamma don't exactly got da mother-daughter love t'ing nailed.'

Tokes was still walking backwards and he was staring at me in a confused sort of way. Pea had a massive grin on his face.

'I hate my mum,' I said quietly.

'Told you!' said Pea. 'An' what I hear, your dad not around no more neither. I right?'

'My dad's cool,' I muttered. 'My mum drove him away.'

'See! Da Pea know everyt'ing!' said Pea excitedly.

Tokes looked like he was about to ask me something, but then Pea stopped suddenly. We were outside Choudhary's Electrical Store. The sign said: *TVs, stereos, PCs and electrical. Sales and upgrades.*

The Choudharys who own the store lived down the road from us and were probably the only friendly shopkeepers in the whole of Coronation Road. They were also the only people I'd really got to know – until I met Tokes that is. There was a power cut on the street once and my mum wasn't around so I knocked on loads of the neighbours' doors to see if they had any candles and the Choudharys were the only ones who were home. When they found out I was on my own, they invited me in and Mrs Choudhary gave me sweet honey cake while Mr

Choudhary talked to me about Islam and high-definition cameras. He showed me how to use his old Super 8 camera and admitted that he used to be a bit of an amateur film-maker himself.

'In my younger days I fancied myself the next Hitchcock!' he said, laughing through his big furry moustache and offering me more sticky cake.

I remember that their front room smelt of incense and paprika and happiness. There was an old grandma who sat in an armchair by the window and didn't say much, just nodded and smiled, and an assortment of daughters and sisters and aunts who came and went while I was there – all smiling, all dressed in beautiful, glimmering silks.

And then, right at the end, their son – the one I can see behind the counter now – came in. His name was Ishmael and he looked a bit like a Bollywood heart-throb, even though his hair was going a bit thin on top. He wasn't very old, early twenties maybe, and I remember he was wearing cricket whites with big grass stains on the knees. When he offered me his hand to shake, I blushed and all the words in my head disappeared. Then the lights came back on and I realised I was still holding his hand and staring up into his dark black Bollywood eyes. Later he walked me back to our house and my heart was beating so fast as I said thank you that the words came out all in the wrong order.

Mr Choudhary and I have sort of become friends since then. I pop into the shop most days when I'm at home and we discuss the latest cameras he's got in stock. Once Mr Choudhary showed me a film of Ishmael playing cricket. I can still see him, arm raised, red ball in hand, running towards the camera, looking right at me. 'Like a young Shoaib Akhtar,' his father said. 'Only with less hair.'

Ishmael always says hello to me very politely and occasionally he tries to chat to me, but I always go red and can't look at him properly. Something about his eyes makes my knees go weak and my stomach all wobbly.

Anyway, Pea had stopped outside the shop and his face was pressed up against the grille. My stomach did a little flip when I saw Ishmael behind the counter and I could feel my ears going red and hoped the others hadn't noticed. But Pea wasn't even looking at me. He and Tokes were staring at the TV screens in the window. They were all showing images of hooded figures being herded into police vans. The headline beneath said, *Rival gangs fight on Starfish Estate. Gang member rushed to hospital in a critical condition.*

Pea's eyes were glued to the screens and a slow grin had spread across his face. 'See – Shiv's cousin Pats made da news! He like totes famous now, innit!'

Then another headline ran across the bottom of the screen: *Family of injured youth claims he was beaten up by police.*

'Seriously?' said Tokes, turning to Pea, whose eyes were bright with excitement.

'What did I tell you?' Pea hissed under his breath. 'World War Three!'

'Did you know about this?' said Tokes. 'Is this what you told Shiv? That the police hurt Pats?'

Pea looked up and grinned, but I never got to hear his answer because just then a blast of music sounded from his pocket and he pulled out a vivid pink, jewel-encrusted phone from his grubby jeans and flicked it open.

'Yeah?' he said into the handset. 'Yeah, I seen it . . . Good, innit? You what? Now? OK. OK – I said OK, all right, innit.'

Then he flicked the phone shut and I caught the look in his eyes – they reminded me of old Mrs Choudhary's, clouded and almost unseeing. But he grinned at me and Tokes and said, ''S been a blast, but I gotta shoot. Guess I see ya around – if you still alive that is.'

Then he turned and legged it back up Coronation Road towards the station, nearly slipping on a bucket of icy water spilling out of the butcher's, before crashing into an old lady with a shopping trolley.

'Keep filmin', Hollywood,' he called as me and Tokes stood watching him skedaddle. 'Things gonna kick off big time in this hood, I tellin' you!'

Then he dodged into an alleyway and was gone.

'He's mental that kid,' said Tokes. 'And he's gonna get himself killed one day if he keeps hanging out with the Starfish Gang,' he added, a worried look in his eyes.

'Maybe he'll get us killed too,' I said, self-conscious again suddenly now it was just the two of us.

'He's gonna try his best, that's for sure,' said Tokes. His face broke into another sunny grin. 'In the meantime, do you want to, you know, hang out with me for a bit?' he asked. 'Maybe we could, um, do some stuff for your film. If you want to.'

It was funny how he said that. Funny in the way things are when you look back on them after other stuff has happened. If I'd known how things were going to turn out, would I have walked away? Anyway, I didn't. I just shrugged and said, 'OK. If you want.'

'Cool,' he said. 'Where do you want to go?'

SCENE 6: BEHIND THE FISH FACTORY

Next to Coronation Road Station, between the fish factory and a derelict house that looks like a squat, is an abandoned patch of yard. I found it the summer before last when my mum and dad were arguing all the time and I needed somewhere to escape to. But I'd never taken anyone else there before.

We clambered through the hole in the corrugated-iron fence and into the overgrown backyard. It was right behind the station platform and we could hear the announcer going on about some delayed train in a tinny, bored voice. There were so many pigeons roosting up in the netting under the arches that the brickwork was almost completely painted in white pigeon poo, and the stench of fish from the factory was mixed with the smell of old wee and diesel and oil.

But there was an old sofa there, and I'd dragged some other stuff in too: a couple of pots which I'd planted pansies and daisies in, a camping table with only three legs and some faded bunting left over from the Olympics. Tokes looked around him and grinned like I'd just brought him into some kind of palace or something. 'Cool!' he said.

'You like it?' I asked shyly.

He looked at me and smiled his big smile – all white teeth and twinkly eyes. A proper hero's smile. 'I love it!'

'You'll be able to stay out of trouble here,' I said. 'And they'll never find us.'

He looked up, alarmed, and his voice was sharp, like I'd pressed on a place that hurt. 'Who won't find us?'

'Um . . . Shiv and his gang – the Starfish,' I stammered. 'That's all I meant. I . . .'

'Oh.' Tokes seemed to relax. 'Them.' And the way he said it, I wondered who he thought I was talking about. 'I reckon they always track you down in the end,' he said, flopping down on the sofa and looking upwards towards the platform. 'How'd you find this place anyway?'

'I have a lot of spare time,' I said with a shrug. 'And I need somewhere no one else knows about.'

'Because of your mum and dad?'

I could feel the weird clicky feeling in my throat that I get when I have to think about what happened, but luckily there was no time to answer because I could hear the sound of a train overhead. 'Duck!' I yelled, grabbing an old umbrella from behind the sofa. 'It sounds like a through train.'

'What?' said Tokes as I slid on the sofa next to him and pulled the umbrella over both our heads.

'You'll see!'

I was pressed up so tight against Tokes I could smell a faint tang of sweat and toothpaste. As the train went thundering through the station above us, suddenly all the pigeons up in the arches started flying about and making a load of noise, and splats of poo fell all around us.

'The trains make the pigeons poop,' I yelled.

'Like poo rain!' he shouted over the clamour of the train and we both laughed.

'Does that happen often?' asked Tokes, grinning from ear to ear once the train had passed.

'About every ten minutes,' I said.

He laughed. 'This is one weird place to hang out, film girl!'

I shoved the umbrella down the back of the sofa.

'So you want to tell me about your mum?' he asked.

I wasn't expecting that.

'I mean, it must be kind of weird having a mum who's in the government or whatever,' he said. 'It's sort of cool though.'

'It's not cool at all.'

'Why? I mean, she gets to make the law. She can change stuff – make things better. That's good, right?'

I bit my lip and tried to explain. 'I think she cares more about "society" than her own family.'

Tokes didn't say anything, but I could feel his eyes watching me.

'And she only pretends to care about that stuff anyway. All that really matters to her is her career.' I wasn't sure why I was telling him this, and my voice came out a bit funny as I spoke. 'That's why they split up. My mum and dad.'

'Because of her job?'

'Because she puts her career ahead of everything else,' I said. I remember hearing Dad say that, saying he'd had enough of coming in second place to Downing Street. That was the day he walked out. My funny, brilliant, kind dad who left because of her.

'So it was your dad who left?' Tokes said.

'Last year.'

'And you figure that's your mum's fault?'

I nodded.

Tokes glanced up. He had the questioning look in his eyes again. 'You ever talk to her about it?' he asked.

I shrugged. 'No point.'

Tokes nodded, then after a second he said, 'You should put it in your film then – maybe.'

'Maybe,' I said, although I couldn't imagine what my mum would do if I said stuff about her in my film and then it won the competition and got shown on TV – which was part of the prize.

‘You miss your dad?’ Tokes asked.

‘Lots.’ I looked up. ‘He’s funny. And he doesn’t nag. He gets me. She doesn’t.’

‘You see him much?’

‘No. He’s in New York now. He sends me stuff all the time and we Skype sometimes.’ I pushed to the back of my mind the thought that we hadn’t spoken for over two weeks. ‘I’m going to go over there soon, he says. We don’t have a date yet, but . . .’

‘But it’s not the same?’

I nodded. Nothing was the same since my dad left.

Tokes’s forehead wrinkled. ‘That’s something we got in common then.’

‘What? Your dad is abroad too?’

‘Sort of.’ He didn’t look up when he said that, just changed the subject. ‘So we gonna make this film or what?’

I tugged my camera out of my pocket, nervous suddenly. ‘I should probably interview you,’ I muttered.

‘Me?’

‘It’s just you’re sort of the main character now,’ I murmured shyly. ‘You know, like the hero. Because of what happened in the park.’

‘Don’t be dumb,’ he laughed, then his face was serious suddenly. ‘I’m the opposite of a hero – trust me.’

‘The way I see it, you’re the hero, Shiv is the villain and

Little Pea is the funny man,' I said. 'It all kind of fits.'

'And what does that make you?' he asked, squinting at me in the sunlight.

I shrugged. 'The geeky weirdo, I suppose.'

'She usually turns out to be the star in the end,' he said with a smile. 'Doesn't she?'

'Not in my case.'

Tokes gave me another of his funny looks then he shook his head and scuffed his feet against the rubbly ground, sending up clouds of dust. 'And you're really gonna let Pea be in the film?'

'He's good to watch,' I said.

'Yeah, but why does he want to be in it?' said Tokes. 'A kid like that doesn't do anything unless there's something in it for him.'

'Maybe he just likes performing.'

'Maybe,' said Tokes, unconvinced. He glanced up at the pigeons in the netting. 'Anyway, we've got no choice now, because if we don't let him be in it he'll try to mess it up for us.'

'Really?'

He nodded. 'Yeah. And if he is in it he'll probably try to sabotage it anyway! So either way he's bad news.'

I glanced at Tokes again when he said 'sabotage'. I liked the way he used words.

'I know kids like him,' he said. 'Magnets for trouble. Can't help it. They ruin all the good stuff that happens to them.'

'Maybe he wants a fresh start,' I said.

'Maybe,' said Tokes, but his eyes were clouded with doubt.

'Well, maybe he just wants to be friends. It doesn't seem like he has any. Except Shiv and the Starfish Gang.'

'And they're not the kind of friends a kid like that needs,' said Tokes. 'Believe me, I know.'

I wanted to ask him how he knew, but he had the faraway look in his eyes again.

'So can I interview you?' I said instead.

His eyes came back to me and he gave me a look, then said, 'OK. Fine. I'll try to be heroic!'

So I pressed a button and the camera beeped into record mode. It looked good: the skinny kid with the sunshine face, sitting on the ripped-up old sofa, with the graffiti and the corrugated iron and the pansies in pots behind him. There was a shaft of dusty sunlight spilling down from the platform above, drawing lines of light through his fuzzy Afro hair.

I waited for him to say something, but he didn't.

'So, um, tell me about yourself,' I said, putting on a voice like one of those chat-show hosts. 'Er, what are your hobbies?'

'I like football,' he said, uncomfortable suddenly now that the gaze of the lens was turned on him. So I turned the camera down to focus on his feet. His wrecked Vans fitted in with the broken rubble and rubbish scattered all around the den. In the scorching heat the bits of broken glass glowed and looked like they were ready to combust. I moved round in an arc then brought the camera back to focus on his face again.

'Anything else?'

'Books,' he said, still self-conscious. 'I like reading.'

'What sort of books?'

'All sorts,' he said. 'Whatever I can get my hands on. My English teacher, Miss Kayacan, she –' He hesitated like he'd said something he shouldn't, but then he went on. 'Anyway, she reckoned I should read some of the classics. Said I should go to the library over the holidays. Only . . .' He stopped again. 'Only you saw what happened there because you were following me.' He shrugged and looked right at the camera.

'What else?' I asked.

'I like school. I want to get a good education.' He was more serious now, looking down at the rubble, not at the camera. 'For my mum, you know? She reckons education gives you choices in life. That's why we moved –' He broke off again. It was like he was monitoring everything he said.

So I took a deep breath before I asked, 'So, um, are you going to tell me where you were before then?'

He didn't jump down my throat this time. 'Are you gonna put this in the film?'

'I don't have to,' I said.

He looked up at the arches then back at the camera.

'It's nowhere really. Just some place in North London, like Pea said.'

'So why did you move to Coronation Road?'

He sighed then stared hard at me, his face screwed up. Then he seemed to make up his mind about something. 'Can you keep a secret?' he asked.

I nodded. 'I don't have anyone to tell secrets to.'

He grinned but still looked uncertain. 'OK, well, if I tell you this, you have to swear to keep it between me and you.' He looked dead serious as he said, 'Promise?'

I nodded quickly.

'And you can't film it either,' he said.

'OK.' I switched off my camera and waited for him to go on.

'So, my dad,' he said quietly, looking down at his Vans, his face seemed younger suddenly. 'The thing is that he was in with the wrong crowd. My mum was worried I'd get dragged in too.'

'Why?'

'It's hard to explain,' he said, a concentrated expression on his face. 'But basically stuff happened and one day my mum packed up and we left.'

'What did your dad say?'

'He didn't know,' said Tokes quickly. 'We went in the middle of the night so he wouldn't be able to follow us.'

I didn't know what to say so I just kept quiet, let him keep talking.

'My dad's not a bad man,' he said, looking up at me now like it was important to him that I believed this. 'When I was a kid, he taught me how to do keepie-uppies, and how to do wheelies on my bike and all that stuff – he even helped me with my homework when he could, even though he wasn't too hot on school himself. And he treated my mum good too.'

'Why did she leave him then?'

I thought of my dad saying, 'When you're older, you'll understand why I'm going, Maggie.' I wondered if it was the same for Tokes.

He shook his head. 'I don't even know why I'm telling you all this,' he said.

'You don't have to if you don't want to,' I said.

'I kind of do,' he admitted. 'It's sort of a relief to tell someone about it, you know?'

I nodded because I knew exactly how it felt to have secrets eating away at your insides. And maybe that's why he told me, because he could tell I got it – sort of.

'OK, so it's hard to explain. My dad was in this gang. A bit like the Starfish, I suppose.' He hesitated. 'He wanted to get out, make a new start. But once you're into all that it's hard to break free.'

'Right,' I said quietly.

'My mum didn't want that for me.' He looked like there was a kind of weight on him as he spoke, pressing on his shoulders. 'She gave up everything so I could make something of my life. Which is why I can't let her down.'

I wished I'd still been filming then, so I could have zoomed in on his eyes, focused on the bitter black colour in them as he spoke.

'Do you miss him?' I said eventually. 'Your dad?'

He nodded. 'Yeah. He was cool. Funny. Kind.'

I thought of my own dad then: how he could always make me laugh; how he got me in a way my mum never did.

'Every time I hear some black man's been shot or in hospital I always think it could be him.' Tokes's brow was furrowed and he had that 'Do you understand?' look in his eyes, so I nodded even though I didn't understand. Not that bit. Not really.

'You know what the average life expectancy is for a black man involved in gang culture?' he said suddenly.

I shook my head.

'Twenty-eight,' he said. Then he looked down again. 'My dad's thirty-two already. He's been running with the gang since he was fifteen, so he's already pushed his luck, right?'

I imagined filming figures. A two and an eight. Maybe cut out of newspaper or on somebody's front door: 28.

'He's not a bad person, my dad,' Tokes said again, like he

really wanted to make sure I got it. 'He just got in with the wrong crowd. Like Pea, I suppose.'

'So do you think he'll come looking for you?'

Tokes nodded his head. 'Probably. It's not really such a big city. He's gonna find us sooner or later, isn't he?'

I looked at him through the viewfinder. His pebble eyes were dark and thoughtful.

'What'll happen then?'

Tokes face puckered, like he was holding something inside. 'I don't know.'

'And that's why you want to stay away from Shiv and the Starfish Gang,' I said.

He looked up and caught my eye, his face clearing as he said, 'I've got to stay out of trouble. Otherwise my mum's done all this for nothing.'

I remember him saying that, as clear as if I had it on camera. Just as if he knew what would happen all along.

SCENE 7: MAGGIE'S HOUSE

Tokes said we needed to film at my house. 'Contrasts,' he said. 'Miss Kayacan reckons you need contrasts in stories because it makes people really notice stuff. I reckon it must be the same in films too.'

So I took him back to my house, but as soon as we got there I wished I hadn't because I could see right away what he was thinking. We live in this massive, white, double-fronted Georgian mansion with electric gates and a Range Rover parked on a perfect gravel drive out front. Tokes's eyes nearly popped out of his head as he took it all in.

'Do you want to come in?' I asked, pausing by the front door, my face flame-red.

'Um, yeah – sure,' he said.

I let us in. 'Hi. It's only me,' I called as we stepped into the hallway.

'Is someone home?' he asked, looking around nervously like we were in some kind of museum.

'Only the au pair.'

'Au pair?'

'She sort of looks after me,' I said awkwardly. 'We get a different one practically every holiday. This one's called Petra.'

'Will she mind me being here?' he asked, talking in a whisper.

'Petra doesn't care much what I do,' I said. 'She spends most of her time on Skype to the Czech Republic.'

'Oh,' he said again. He was acting totally different in our house; even his voice had changed. He was still standing motionless on the doormat. 'Should I take my shoes off?' he asked, glancing at the polished wood flooring.

No shoes in the house – that's one of my mum's favourite rules.

'No,' I said. 'Keep them on.'

I led the way into the kitchen which is a huge room at the back of the house with a glass roof and chrome surfaces and a big island in the middle, covered with gleaming appliances.

Tokes let out a little laugh when we stepped into it.

'What's funny?' I asked.

'It's just . . . this is twice as big as our whole bedsit.'

'Oh, right,' I said, wishing again that I hadn't brought him.

'Do you want something to eat?' I asked. 'I can get Petra to make a sandwich if you like.'

He was staring at the shiny red fridge with an expression on his face like he was really hungry, but he just said, 'Nah, I'm good.'

'You sure?'

'I said I'm good.' He looked odd when he said that, like he was suddenly mad at me or something.

'You've got to have a Krispy Kreme doughnut then.' I grabbed a box out of the fridge and put it down on the kitchen island. 'My dad sends me a dozen every week.'

Tokes had been gazing up at the glass roof of the kitchen, and out at the garden, but he turned round and stared at the tray of multicoloured glazed doughnuts – pink ones and white ones and one with sprinkles and toffee cubes. 'Seriously?' he said. 'A whole box?'

I shrugged and tried to explain. 'It's because I loved them when I was little. Once I ate so many, I was sick.' I paused, remembering the smell of vomit and doughnuts and shame. Then I said, 'I think they're to make up for him not being around, you know?'

'So do you eat them all?'

I shook my head. 'I usually end up throwing half of them away.'

'In that case . . .' Tokes took a doughnut and bit into it like he hadn't eaten properly for days. 'Seems silly to waste them!' he said, his mouth full of chewy dough. He was looking round the kitchen again, taking in all the framed photos on the walls.

'It feels like we're a million miles from Coronation Road in here,' he said. 'Shiv and the Starfish Gang and Little Pea – it's like none of that other stuff even exists. Like it can't touch you.'

'I suppose,' I said.

'Is this your mum?' he asked, pointing at a picture of a tall, dark-haired woman in a striking red suit, shaking hands with Tony Blair.

'Yeah,' I said. 'And that one.' I pointed at a picture of my mum talking to the Queen and the Duke of Edinburgh. She loves that photo.

'It is pretty cool, you've got to admit,' said Tokes, looking impressed.

'I told you. There is nothing cool about my mum,' I said quietly. The sad face on my right boot seemed to glower up at me as I said it. Like it was accusing me of lying.

Just then the kitchen door opened and a young woman with dark black eye make-up and blonde hair with black roots stuck her head round the door.

'Hi, Petra,' I muttered.

She didn't seem that interested. She just nodded, taking in the sight of Tokes and me and the box of doughnuts without comment. 'Your mother call,' she said in heavily accented English.

'What did she want?'

'She not home till late tonight. She say eat without her.'

I shot Tokes a look as Petra made her way over to the fridge and started pulling stuff out. I've filmed her quite a bit without her knowing it, but she's one of those people who don't give much away. She looked up with lazy eyes and said, 'Your friend want to stay for dinner?'

'No,' said Tokes quickly.

I glanced at him. He was looking uncomfortable again. 'Come on,' I said. 'Let's find somewhere else to film.'

I filmed Tokes as he checked out our house. I've got footage of him pushing open doors and peeking into other rooms. The toilet made him laugh. 'It's the size of a footie pitch,' he said, taking in the golden taps and the black-and-white pictures all over the crimson red walls. 'Who needs a loo this big?'

He reckoned my mum's office looked like something from a stately home. Then he opened the door to the sitting room, which is all leather sofas and glass tables and two walls covered from floor to ceiling in books. 'Whoa!' He stood staring at the bookshelves. I caught his face on camera – eyes lit up like the words were pouring out of the books and making his skin tingle. 'It's like having a library in your own house.'

'My mum gets mad because I never read them,' I said as he ran his hands up and down the leather spines.

'You don't like reading?' He pulled his eyes away from the books for a second to look at me.

I shrugged. 'I don't get on so well with books.'

'My dad is like that,' he said. 'Me, I love them. Better even than doughnuts, you know!' He grinned.

'You want to borrow one?' I asked quickly.

He glanced at the books again, a look of longing in his eyes. 'Nah,' he said. 'I'm OK.'

'But nobody reads them – it seems a shame.'

He stared at the shelf. Some of the books looked so old they must have been printed a hundred years ago. They were sort of beautiful – all the shades of fading leather and gold embossed lettering. My dad ordered them alphabetically and I remember my mum calling him obsessive-compulsive. I think they had a big row about that too.

Tokes pulled out a copy of a leather-bound book which said *Great Expectations* in gold lettering along the spine. 'Miss Kayacan said I should read this,' he said. 'I tried to take it out of the library.' He looked up, his eyes distant, underwater, like he was already thinking about somewhere else. 'Are you sure your mum won't mind?'

'You can keep it for all she'll notice.'

'No, I'll bring it back,' said Tokes firmly. 'As soon as I've read it.'

Just then my phone beeped and I looked down at it.

'It's a text. From Pea,' I said.

'How did he get your number?'

'I have no idea.' I remembered Pea saying he knew everything that went down on Coronation Road, but no one around here even knows my name, let alone my number.

'What does he say?' Tokes looked worried again.

'He says he's set up some stuff for us to film.'

Tokes rolled his eyes. 'Should have known.'

'He wants us to meet him tomorrow,' I added. 'Apparently, he's got some well good news to tell us.'

'So much for keeping out of trouble,' said Tokes.

'Do you think we should go?'

'We've got to, haven't we?' said Tokes with a shrug. 'He'll tell Shiv about your film otherwise.'

'*You* don't have to come though.' I looked at him nervously, remembering what he'd said about keeping out of trouble.

'I can't let you go on your own,' he said. 'You don't know how it works with kids like Pea and Shiv.'

'I don't need you to look after me,' I said.

'I know,' said Tokes. 'But neither of us wants any trouble. And we're mates, aren't we?'

My stomach contracted oddly and I looked at him hard to see if he was kidding. 'I guess,' I said.

'Well, mates look out for each other,' he said with a smile. 'So we're in this together, OK?'

I nodded. And I think I felt happier in that moment than I had for months.

SCENE 8: OUTSIDE MAGGIE'S BEDROOM

My mum got back really late that night. I heard her coming in long after midnight, her heels clip-clipping on the wooden floor (she never keeps her own rules), talking on her mobile phone.

'I'm talking to Channel 4 News tomorrow,' I heard her saying as she reached the foot of the stairs. 'Yes, I know this is very sensitive, Adrian . . . yes, I understand what's at stake.'

There was a long pause, then the footsteps started to make their way up the stairs – I could tell from the different sound they made on the carpet. 'We cannot have the public thinking that Pats Karunga was beaten up in police custody.' She stops briefly. 'If this gets out, it'll cause a riot.'

She was halfway up the stairs and I could see her through the open doorway of my bedroom. I flicked on my camera and caught her standing there.

She looked beautiful in the lamplight. My mum doesn't

look anything like me, except she's small without her giant heels on. She's all raven-black hair, red lipstick, crisp-cut suits and designer shoes, like some kind of newsreader. People describe her as 'striking' and 'stunning'. Me, I'm more like my dad: wispy strawberry-blonde hair (when it isn't purple or pink or green or whatever), a face like a mixture between a frog and a pixie (my dad's words!), twiggy arms and legs, and skin so pale you can almost see through me. People sometimes say I'm 'sweet' or 'cute', but never 'beautiful'.

It's easy to say who my mum would be if she was in a film. She's the beautiful villainess type, you know, like Cruella de Vil or the Queen in *Snow White*. So beautiful you start off thinking she's a nice person until you get drawn in and it's too late: you're already under her spell and you can't stop staring at her.

'Karunga's family are claiming he was uninjured when he got in that police van,' she was saying.

I remembered the running headline on the TV screens in Choudhary's Electrical Store: *Family of injured youth claims he was beaten up by police.*

'So do we actually know how he arrived at King's College Hospital with a cracked skull and punctured lung?'

She turned her head in my direction as she spoke, but she didn't seem to notice that my door was open. That I was awake. Watching her as she listened to the answer.

'OK, fine. So for the moment the official line will be that Pats Karunga is a known gang member with a criminal record. That the police were called in to break up a fight between rival gangs. That Karunga was carrying a weapon, yes?'

The pause seemed to shimmer in the night air. 'Yes, I understand. I'll make it clear that we have full confidence in the police. In the meantime, I want anything you can find that will deflect press attention away from police involvement, OK?'

I could hear myself breathing; and for the second time in two days I had a feeling I'd filmed something I shouldn't.

'Relations between the community and the police are strained enough around here,' she went on. 'And I do not want a riot on my hands.' She ran a hand through her dark hair and again her eyes strayed in my direction, but didn't seem to see me.

'Yes . . . yes . . . I understand that, Adrian, but sometimes the truth has to come second to matters of public security.' I have her on film saying that. Paused on the stairway, phone to her ear, a clock chiming somewhere in the background.

Then she hung up and just stood there for a moment, staring straight ahead, a concentrated look in her eyes. Was she worried? Upset? Then the look was gone and she smoothed her hair and made her way up the stairs.

I quickly flicked my camera off and shoved it under my pillow.

'Hi, Mum,' I called as she passed in front of my open doorway.

'God! Maggie! You made me jump!' She turned so that she was framed by the doorway like a portrait, blinking like she was tired or that she'd forgotten she even had a daughter. 'What are you doing up at this time?'

'I couldn't sleep,' I muttered.

She took a couple of steps into my room. Out of the light she looked different, her features softer in the gloom. 'Look, Maggie, I've had a long day,' she sighed wearily.

For a second I wanted to warn her. Or to ask for her help. But I didn't do either.

I just said, 'I know that boy.'

'Who?' She wasn't really looking at me. Her phone had just beeped and she was reading a message on the screen.

'The boy in hospital. The one you say got beaten up by the police.'

She looked up then. 'Really! How do you know him exactly?' She ran her finger over the nape of her neck which she only ever does when she's feeling uncomfortable. I've filmed her so much that I know all her little mannerisms.

'I just know some people who know him.'

'Right.' She took another couple of steps into the room and perched on the end of my bed. I pulled up my feet and wrapped my arms round my knees so that we weren't touching. 'Well, you must have misheard me because he was not beaten by the police.' She looked at me, her eyes straying over my face. She smiled, sighed and said, 'And, to be honest, I'd rather you kept your distance from boys like that.' I wondered if Petra had told her about Tokes coming over. 'They are not particularly good news.'

'But that doesn't make it OK for the police to hurt him,' I said.

She exhaled. 'No, it doesn't. If that's even what happened, which I don't believe it was.'

'He's got the same rights as anyone else, hasn't he?'

'Yes,' she said. 'Of course he has.'

'Well then? That's what you do, isn't it? Defend people's rights. Uphold the law.' I remembered Tokes saying that earlier. For some reason I wanted him to be right. For her to agree with what he'd said.

She looked at me in that way she sometimes does. Like she needs to protect me, like I don't know anything. 'Sometimes things are more complicated than they seem, Maggie.'

'I don't see how. Dad says . . .'

She cut me off then and the softness went out of her eyes. 'Your father said a lot of things.' Her eyes were brighter suddenly. 'But sometimes actions speak louder than words. When you're a bit older, perhaps you'll understand that.'

'I'm old enough to know what a cover-up is!' I said, my face hot, and tears too close.

Her brow furrowed. 'Look, Maggie, it's late and I don't want to argue with you about this, OK?' Her eyes tried to find mine again, but I looked away. 'However, you need to understand that this is a very politically sensitive issue so whatever you *think* you may have overheard, I'd rather you didn't go spreading silly rumours which will just cause trouble for everyone.'

Especially you, I thought to myself.

She sat for a moment, still looking at me. I didn't meet her eye. She stood up and looked as if she was about to move off, then she stopped and smiled. 'I like your hair,' she said. 'Did you dye it again?'

I managed the barest of nods.

She smiled again. 'It's cool, Maggie.'

I might have looked up and smiled then, but her phone beeped and I'd lost her attention. She turned to go, pulling the door closed behind her. She blew me a kiss as she went, but I could hear her talking as she moved into her room. And she might only have been next door, but I knew she was miles away from me.

SCENE 9: THE NEXT MORNING. CHOUDHARY'S ELECTRICAL STORE

It was early and Mr Choudhary had only just pulled up the grille to open the store, but the sun was already vicious and the weather map on the six screens in the window was dotted with sunshine and soaring numbers.

'Welcome, Maggie!' beamed Mr Choudhary when he saw me. 'You are very welcome. Very welcome.'

Ishmael was adjusting the window display. He nodded and smiled when he saw me and I tried to do the same, but ended up going bright red and tripping over my boots as I stepped into the shop.

'What can I do for you this morning, Miss Maggie?' asked Mr Choudhary, his moustache glistening in the heat and his eyes twinkling. 'No new stock to show you today, I'm afraid.'

'I was, um, wondering if you could help me with something, Mr Choudhary.'

I'd been thinking about this last night when I'd been trying to get to sleep, the images of the last two days tripping on an endless flickering loop through my head. I figured I needed to do this right away, before anything else happened – before Shiv found out about my secret footage or something – and I reckoned Mr Choudhary was the only person who could help.

'If I can help you, I most certainly will, my friend.' He always talked in this formal way, like I was an adult, not a skinny fourteen-year-old, like we were in one of the black-and-white films he loved so much.

'I'm trying to work out if there's a way of syncing my camera with my laptop,' I said.

'For what purpose, may I enquire?' he asked, running a finger thoughtfully over his moustache.

'I'm making this film, you see,' I explained. 'For a competition. And I'm worried that if I lost my camera or I was mugged and it got stolen –'

'Indeed, indeed!' He nodded sagely. 'More robberies, more break-ins in Coronation Road than ever in my lifetime, Miss Maggie! We have been here for twenty years – family business, you see – and in that time we have seen many changes. The crime rate is worse than ever. I tell my wife and daughters not to walk out on the streets alone after dark.' He shook his head.

From over by the window Ishmael caught my eye and

smiled, which he often did when his father started talking like this. He looked more like a movie star than ever this morning. I felt the colour in my cheeks soar and I looked away quickly.

'Ack, forgive an old man for rambling on,' Mr Choudhary said. 'You were asking me about your camera, yes?'

'Yes, I – I mean, do you think it's possible?'

'I can do it.' It was Ishmael who spoke. He came over to join us by the counter and he was standing so close I could smell the sharp musky tang of his deodorant, see the dark hairs on his bare arms.

I gave a little shiver and tried very, very hard to keep my voice normal as I said, 'Oh, can you?'

'Ah yes. Best to ask Ishmael,' said Mr Choudhary. 'My son has outstripped me when it comes to technology, Miss Maggie. It is the way of the world for sons to overtake their old fathers!'

Ishmael rolled his eyes at me again like we were both in on some joke. I bit my lip and tried to smile back.

'You have your laptop?' asked Ishmael in the kindly big-brother voice he always used to address me.

I nodded quickly.

'Right, I will leave you in my son's capable hands and I will be the tea-wallah!' Mr Choudhary laughed then went into the back of the shop to make us all a cup.

I stood awkwardly, pretending to look at a display of

cameras while Ishmael installed the new settings on my computer. I kept sneaking little peaks at him as he tapped away at the keyboard, an expression of concentration in his dark black eyes. Mr Choudhary continued to go on about the state of Coronation Road through the bead curtain that separated the counter from the back of the shop.

'Maybe your mother can do something about it. Gangs roaming the streets, dealing drugs on street corners, carrying weapons some of them.'

I glanced at the large TVs on display in the window. They were set to the twenty-four-hour news channel and a headline in red at the top read *Breaking News*. On-screen, a senior police officer was making a statement outside Scotland Yard and the running headline below said, *Met deny rumours of police cover-up*. Then, *Local MP calls Karunga a 'known member of the criminal underworld'*.

'There, you see – more crime in Coronation Road,' said Mr Choudhary, reappearing with cups of sweet tea in Lord's Cricket Ground mugs. 'Ishmael tells me that boy Pats was in his class at school, and now look at him. Terrible – ack!'

Ishmael was running through footage from my camera – stuff I'd filmed yesterday. I turned and saw an image of my mother on the screen. It was on mute, but I remembered her saying, 'Sometimes the truth has to come second to matters of public security.'

'Does it work?' I asked hastily, wondering what else he'd seen.

'I think so,' said Ishmael. He looked up and eyed me curiously. I wanted to explain about the footage in the park, but I knew I couldn't. 'It uploads automatically on to your laptop within a few minutes of you filming. Your footage should be safe no matter what happens to the camera.'

'Excellent!' said Mr Choudhary, clapping his hands and grinning. 'We should do a trial. Film something and see if it arrives on your laptop safely.'

So that's what we did. Me and Mr Choudhary made a movie. He did his best impressions of Robert De Niro and Sean Connery and he finished by saying, 'And this is my son. The best bowler south of the Thames. Better than Tendulkar. Better than Warne.' And he put his arm round Ishmael, who shook his head and rolled his eyes. I've watched that bit a lot – when he makes eye contact with the camera and seems to stare right into it. Right at me. It makes my tummy flip every time.

Afterwards, we checked and, sure enough, the footage had already uploaded on to my laptop, without me having to do anything.

'Will it work anywhere?'

'You could film something on the other side of the world,' said Ishmael, 'and it would be on your laptop at home the next time you switch it on.'

'Wonderful!' said Mr Choudhary, shaking his head in wonder. 'No matter what happens, your blockbuster will be safe, eh? Don't forget us when you win your first Oscar, Miss Maggie!'

SCENE 10: MAGGIE'S DEN

Jeopardy. That's what a great film script needs, according to my favourite movie magazine anyway. It means that there must be an element of risk, a threat to the main protagonists, an obstacle in the way of them achieving their dreams. The audience needs to feel that the characters might lose everything.

Jeopardy is great in movies. And not so good in real life.

I dropped my laptop back home then went round to the den and waited for Tokes like we'd arranged. He didn't turn up for a bit, so I sat on the sofa and looked at some of the footage we'd shot yesterday. It was weird watching myself back. I looked strange – not like myself somehow. Tokes had been holding the camera and it shook a bit and kept going out of focus. I was half in shadow and the camera seemed to look right into my eyes. Like I said before, you can usually tell a lot about people from their eyes, but I couldn't read mine.

There was a rustle on the other side of the fence. I looked up, expecting to see Tokes. A small hand reached through the gap and a grubby piece of paper shot out of it and landed on the rubbly ground. I scrambled forward and ducked my head out just in time to catch sight of Little Pea disappearing under the archway.

'Hey!' I called.

But he just turned and yelled, 'Ran outta credit on my phone, dittn't I!' then legged it under the arches by Coronation Road Station.

I pulled my head back in again quickly and unfolded the scrappy piece of paper, wondering how Pea had found out about the den. Or how he knew my phone number.

Cum 2 youth club 10 o'clock, it said. *Lites, camera, akshun!* Underneath was a little picture of a round pea with a smiley face.

'Um – hi.'

I looked up. Tokes was squeezing through the gap, carrying a parcel wrapped in newspaper.

'You want some chips?' he asked, pushing the greasy package in my direction.

I looked at it uncertainly. 'Where did you get them?'

'It's one of my mum's jobs. She works the night shift in

a burger bar. Brings home chips for breakfast. Or burgers sometimes. Nice, but always cold.'

'Right,' I said. I had a feeling he'd be offended if I said no, so I reached for one and folded it into my mouth. It was cold and lumpy.

'What happened to your hair?' he asked.

I put my hand up to my head. I'd been messing around with it again last night and it was now half purple, half white and a bit spikier on top. 'I fancied a change,' I said.

'It looks, um, good,' he said, plonking down next to me on the sofa and handing me another chip. I nibbled it slowly while Tokes bolted down handfuls and we talked about Pea's note.

'He's letting us know he can find us,' said Tokes, shaking his head. 'That we can't hide from him.'

'Do you think he's told Shiv?' I said. I was busy filming the note, running the camera over the piece of paper, focusing on each word.

'About the den or the film?'

I shrugged. 'Either.'

Tokes shook his head. 'Not yet. Secrets are currency to a kid like that. He'll keep the information till he needs it then he'll spill or keep schtum for the highest bidder.'

'Did you see the stuff on the news?' I asked. 'About Shiv's cousin Pats. Do *you* think it was the police who did it?'

Tokes shrugged. 'Maybe. Or maybe somebody just wants people to think so.'

'Why would they want that?'

'I dunno. To cover up who really did it? To cause trouble? Who knows?'

'My mum said it'll cause a riot if people believe it,' I said.

Tokes nodded his head. 'She could be right. If Pea started the rumour, he's playing with fire.'

I glanced at my watch. 'Do you think we should go see what he's up to?'

'I guess,' said Tokes, but he looked uneasy. 'I don't like it though. I really don't trust that kid.'

Just then a squeaky little voice said, 'Well, that's not a very nice t'ing to say, issit?'

Tokes spun round again as Pea's head appeared over the corrugated-iron fence.

'Mornin', sunshines!' he chirped. He looked weird there. I guessed his legs and the rest of his body were dangling out of sight.

Tokes said nothing for a second, just shook his head, then asked, 'So how did you find us?'

'I tell you yesterday, T-man! I got eyes everywhere in Coronation Road, innit! See everyt'ing. Know everyt'ing. Got ways of findin' out everyt'ing too!' He winked at me when he said that.

'Like my phone number?' I said. 'How did you get that?'

'Ain't you never heard of blue-snarfin', posh girl?' Pea smirked.

'What?' said Tokes, shaking his head.

'Bluetooth piracy, innit. All da best spooks use it. Not my fault if you so way behind da times you easy to hack, girl!' Pea beamed happily then added with a cryptic grin, 'Course, mebbe I jus' nicked your phone an' sent myself a text, old-school-style! You probs should keep it somewhere a bit safer – you a way easy target for pickpockets.'

I patted my pocket suspiciously to check my phone was still there while Tokes tutted. 'You are unbelievable!'

'Hey, you gotta cross da line sometimes when you a super-spy like me,' said Pea. 'An' you be surprised da t'ings I overhear!' He winked at Tokes this time.

'Oh yeah? Like what?' asked Tokes, his jaw clenching.

'Nuttin' much,' said Pea, hauling himself up so his elbows came over the fence. 'Jus' that Hollywood here gone all fifty shades of purple with her hairdo, an' you a North London boy wit' Daddy issues.'

Tokes's face went pale beneath his dark skin and he took an angry step forward. 'How the hell . . .?' Then he stopped and glared at Pea. 'Did you follow us yesterday?'

'Can't reveal my sources!' said Pea with a grin.

'You were spying on us!' said Tokes angrily. Then he shook

his head and stared at Pea with narrowed eyes. 'Well, anything you think you heard about my dad you'd better scrub it from your head,' he said, his voice low and gruff.

Pea giggled nervously and pulled his legs over so he was perched on the fence, feet dangling out, ready for a speedy exit if he needed it. 'Chill out, T-bone!'

Tokes took a step towards him. 'I'm serious! I don't care what else you do, but the stuff about my dad, you best forget it.' Tokes's face was still pale and his eyes were bright. I could see that he was really rattled. 'In fact, why don't you just clear off and leave us alone, OK!'

Pea's face lost its smile for a second. 'But what 'bout da film, T-man? I gonna be a movie star, remember?'

'Don't call us, we'll call you,' Tokes muttered.

'But I want in.' Pea turned to stare at me and his eyes were like a little kid's, begging for sweets. 'Come on, peeps, you my only frien's. I ain't got no one else.'

His eyes flicked from me to Tokes and when neither of us said anything he cocked his head again in the weird jerky way he had and his eyes glistened as he said, 'An' I even set up a movie magic moment for you this very mornin'. Peace offerin', you know? You not get my note?'

'We got it,' said Tokes. 'But we figured you were just setting up a load more trouble.'

'No ways! In fact, you be thankin' me later,' grinned

Pea. 'An' I come to tell you I got you a job interview too, alien boy!'

'A job interview?' I said, glancing from Tokes's angry face to Pea's excited one, wondering what on earth Pea was going on about this time.

'Yeah. I figured T-boy here tried to save me from Shiv so da least I could do was re-turn da favour.' He did a little shimmy, like he was on a catwalk, shaking his booty.

'I thought you said you didn't need rescuing,' said Tokes. 'And I don't need any favours.'

Pea suddenly looked cross and upset. 'Well, *she* does,' he said, pointing at me. 'Posh girl ain't got no diplomatic immunity in this hood – don't matter who her mamma is!'

'Just lay off her.' Tokes shook his head angrily. 'What did she ever do to you?'

'I jus' sayin', that's all,' said Little Pea, flipping backwards over the fence so that only his head was visible again. 'I just da messenger, North London boy. An' you know how it works!'

Then he slid down and we just saw a flash of Pea's face as he said, 'Now I gotta go see a man 'bout a police brutality rap. See ya later, peeps? We gonna make cinema history, innit!'

Tokes didn't look at me for a minute. His face was still wrinkled into a frown and he stared hard at the hole in the corrugated-iron fence which Pea had just disappeared through.

'We've been too nice to him,' he mumbled. 'Big mistake.'

'What?'

'Kids like Pea, they only understand one thing.' His eyes looked different suddenly, weary. 'He's so used to everyone in his life beating him up that if you treat him nice he doesn't respect you.'

'But why?' I said. 'That doesn't make any sense.'

Tokes was staring upwards. 'If you get knocked around enough, you don't know any other way of being.'

I thought of the scars on Little Pea's torso and all over his head.

'I guess he can't help being how he is,' Tokes went on. 'But he knows about my dad which means he's got something on me.'

'Maybe he's just bluffing. Maybe he doesn't know anything.'

Tokes shrugged. 'Maybe.'

I hesitated, unsure whether to ask the next question. 'Um, why are you so worried about him knowing about your dad anyway? Is it because you think he'll find him, tell him where you are?'

Tokes's eyes crinkled as he looked up at the sunshine and sighed. 'I know my dad'll find us in the end,' he said. 'But I just want it not to be right away. It took all my mum's strength to leave him. I don't think she could do it again.'

'And you don't *want* to go back?'

Tokes paused again. 'I miss my dad,' he said firmly. 'But no, I don't want to go back.'

I remember thinking it was funny – not laugh-out-loud funny, just odd, I suppose – that all I wanted was for my mum and dad to get back together again. For us to be a family like we used to be. And Tokes wanted the total opposite.

'Is that because you think your mum's right?' I said. 'You think you'll, you know, get caught up in the gang stuff if you go back?'

'Yes,' he said quietly. Then he looked at me uncertainly. 'You know, you might not like me if I told you everything about myself.'

'I probably would,' I said, because I didn't think there was anything Tokes could tell me that would make me not like him.

'And I don't think you'd understand,' he said quietly. 'You come from a different world.'

I looked down at my boots. I'd Tippexed on some more stuff so now the smiley face seemed to wink up at me with its tongue stuck out. 'So we've got to do what Pea says then,' I said. 'We've got no choice. He's got something on both of us now.'

Tokes shook his head again, like he was trying to shake some thought out of his brain.

'And I suppose we can, you know.' I felt awkward saying it.

'Like you said, we can look out for each other, right?'

I stared at him. There was no doubt he was the kind of person you wanted on your side if things all went belly up, but I still wasn't sure why he wanted me for a friend.

But he turned to me and smiled and his face was all sunshine again. 'That'd be cool,' he said.

I blushed happily. 'And I was thinking,' I said, the words tumbling out of my mouth in a rush. 'Maybe if I filmed it, you know, then if anything happens we've got evidence.'

Tokes looked doubtful again. 'I dunno. You're already in enough trouble if Shiv finds out you were filming in the park the other day.'

'But I could do it undercover,' I said quickly. 'I could put the camera in my pocket and cut a hole or something.'

'You reckon that would work?' he asked doubtfully.

I shrugged. 'It might.'

'You don't mind cutting up your clothes?'

I gave him a funny look and he took in my scruffy cut-off boy jeans and *Toy Story* T-shirt and we both grinned. 'OK. I guess not,' he said.

'Have you got some scissors?' I asked.

He shook his head.

'A knife?'

'No!' He shook his head quickly and his jaw tightened. 'I promised my mum I'd never carry a weapon.'

'Sorry – course,' I said, worried I'd offended him.

But Tokes screwed up his face for a second and then broke into a grin. 'Hey! I've got a better idea!'

He rummaged around in his rucksack and pulled out one of those see-through ID label holders that you hang round your neck.

'It's my mum's,' he said. 'From her hospital cleaning job. She thought she'd lost this one, so she got another. What do you reckon?'

I took it off him and slipped my camera into the plastic wallet. It fitted perfectly. 'Won't it be obvious?'

Tokes shrugged. 'Not as obvious as you standing there pointing the lens at people.'

'I guess.' I hung the wallet round my neck and pressed record. 'It might be a bit fuzzy and I don't know if the sound will record.'

'It's open at the top near the microphone bit, so I guess it might work.' Tokes hesitated for a second and looked at me. 'What do you reckon? I mean, Pea's gonna figure it out right away.'

'He might not,' I said hopefully.

'He will,' said Tokes. 'But maybe that's not such a bad thing. He won't want us filming anything that'll get him in trouble. Maybe it'll keep him in line.'

'Maybe,' I said, more doubtful this time.

Tokes looked thoughtful again for a second, then he shrugged and said, 'Come on then, film girl. We've got no choice but to go find out what Little Pea is up to.' He smiled. 'At least, whatever happens, we'll have some good stuff for your movie – when we're both dead!'

SCENE 11: OUTSIDE THE STARFISH PROJECT

A gaggle of teenagers was hanging around outside the Starfish Project youth club. It wasn't open yet and the gates were padlocked shut. There was a high fence with barbed wire on top running all round the building, but it didn't seem to have stopped people painting graffiti all over the brickwork.

The Starfish Project is in one of the railway arches on the other side of the station. There's a whole world under those arches: shoe factories manned by illegal immigrants, artists' studios, a boxing club, a vodka bar and a whole load of warehouses which my dad reckons are filled with stolen goods.

The youth club is in the furthest arch. My mum was always going on about the great work it's doing keeping kids off the streets, but she also told me never to go there.

Little Pea was perched on the high wall outside the club. He looked like he must have flown up because it was twice as high as he was. When he saw us, he didn't jump down, he just nodded at Tokes, who nodded back, and gave me a giant grin.

'Ain't I a great location researcher, Hollywood!' he chirped. 'Look at this place. Be a great backdrop to da scene, right?'

'What scene?' Tokes demanded, looking round at the people waiting, trying to figure out what we were supposed to be there for. 'What do you want from us?'

'Nuttin' yet,' said Pea. 'Just wait though. It be well worth your while.'

'If you say so,' said Tokes.

Pea wiggled his legs. 'Hey! How 'bout I do you a screen test while we waitin'?' He nodded at the camera round my neck, which he'd spotted right away, just like Tokes had said he would.

'I see you gone Undercover Black Ops – that's cool,' he said, in a super-loud whisper. I noticed that the little scars on his head stood out in the sunshine.

'Told you!' said Tokes.

'Does it work in that t'ing?' Pea went on, nodding at the plastic case.

'Um, I haven't tried it yet.'

'Come on then. Let's give it a go. Quick, before they get here.'

'Before who gets here?' Tokes asked suspiciously. 'Don't tell me Shiv's coming?'

'Don't wanna spoil da surprise!' Pea giggled. 'So you gonna film me or what?'

I glanced at Tokes who was shaking his head and looking round angrily. 'Do we have any choice?' I asked.

Pea just smirked so I flicked the camera on and started recording.

'Ask me some questions. Go on!' said Pea, preening at the camera like he was on *America's Next Top Model*.

Tokes wasn't letting him off the hook. 'Have you deliberately led us into some kind of trap?'

'Chill, man!' scolded Little Pea softly. 'An' you be a rubbish interviewer. Your turn, Hollywood!'

I glanced at Tokes who was still scowling. 'Um, so, um, do you go to the youth club?'

When you watch the footage of this bit, Pea looks different because of the shadows falling on him from above. The inside of his mouth is like a pink bud against the chocolate of his face. He looks more like an old man than a little kid. But he grins like he's some Hollywood starlet.

'Nah! My mamma she won't let me,' he says in a voice that has a vaguely American twang to it. 'She reckon this place is in da grip of da devil.'

I turned in a slow circle so that the camera panned away from Pea's face and round the street. It worked too. When you watch that bit back, you can see everything: the way the light fell over the barbed wire; the rubbish skittering down the road like tumbleweed in a cowboy movie. And in the background you can hear Pea's voice going on, 'Yeah, she reckon her and all da peeps at her church needs to come down to this place an' do an exorcism to drive out da bad guy!'

'Your church seriously does exorcisms?' asked Tokes, turning to look at him, an expression in his brown eyes that I hadn't seen before.

Pea shrugged. 'Yeah, all da time, man. Drivin' da devil outta Coronation Road on a daily basis, innit!'

'Who do they do them on then?' I asked.

'Everyone – little kids an' women mostly. When they been misbehavin'! Dittn't work on me though,' said Pea, looking straight at the camera and waggling his eyebrows, like he was kind of proud of himself.

'What exactly do they do in an exorcism anyway?' I asked.

'Sorry, time's up!' Pea declared with another massive grin. 'You want da juice you gotta put a ring on it!'

'What?'

Pea nodded at my camera and said, 'Gotta sign me up for da film before I tell you da whole juicy story. Little Pea don't give away intel for free! Anyway, it time for da real feature presentation now, innit!'

'What?' Tokes spun round and Pea's eyes sparkled like black gems in his round face.

And that was when I noticed that all the kids waiting outside the Starfish Project had gone silent.

'Lights, camera . . .' sang Pea.

I turned round to see what he was looking at and, sure enough, walking towards us from the direction of the station was the Starfish Gang with Shiv at the helm.

Pea giggled some more. 'Some scenes have been set up for your viewin' pleasure,' he parroted. Then he jumped down next to me and whispered loudly, 'Keep it rollin', Hollywood.'

Tokes glared at Pea and whispered, 'You set us up?'

'Genius, innit!'

Shiv was wearing his long leather coat and the light was behind him, so he still looked like a skinny vampire sparkling in the sunshine. Tad's strawberry-blond hair was almost transparent in the glare and his skin glowed ghostly pale.

Shiv caught sight of Tokes and stopped. The other two halted abruptly behind him, and Little Pea went fluttering and hopping over like he was their favourite pet instead of Shiv's punchbag.

'Here he is,' said Pea, gesturing theatrically at Tokes. 'Jus' the man you wanted to see, Shiv-man. Told you I deliver him, dittn't I!'

Shiv was already staring at Tokes. And Tokes was staring at Shiv. It was like a gangster movie; it felt like it needed a bit of slidy metallic music in the background and lots of long, slow mood shots. The camera was still rolling in the pouch around my neck, but I had no idea if I was filming anything.

Shiv took a step forward and addressed Tokes like no one else was around. 'You and me need to talk, boy.'

The heat was suffocating, but I felt a shiver go down my spine and I felt sick with the taste of cold chips and fear.

'I don't have anything to talk to you about,' Tokes said. Somehow he managed to seem totally cool. It was almost like he didn't really care what happened to him and that gave him some kind of weird advantage.

Shiv took another step forward, irritated. 'You know who you talkin' to, boy?'

'Should I?' Tokes responded.

It was Tad who replied. 'We know all about you, North-of-the-River boy!' He was grinning, his pale blue eyes swimming with laughter.

Beside me I felt Tokes stiffen. I looked over at Pea who just shrugged his shoulders, like he was saying, 'You can't expect me to keep every little secret, can you?'

'Little bird say you mebbe the Tottenham crew – I right?' Tad's long body looked like a strawberry lace; his trousers hung so low they were nearly down to his knees. But it was like menace sweated out of his pores, filling the air with the scent of it.

Tokes didn't say anything as Little Pea flapped his arms like wings and said, 'Word spreads, T-man!'

'Same little bird also say you on da run from yo daddy,' said Shiv, who was motionless, staring at Tokes with a hungry look in his eyes. 'You don't wanna be found. That right?'

'Supposing it is?' said Tokes. I wished I could focus in on his eyes then: they seemed as black and hard as Shiv's, but with determination, not malice.

'You not hear what happen to bluds from other crews what step into da wrong hood?' said Tad from Shiv's side.

In my head I could already see the scene on film: the camera moving from one face to the other, catching the long pauses; the blazing sun beating down on the tarmac so that it bubbles with heat; the air white-hot with tension.

'Yeah, I know,' said Tokes, meeting Tad's gaze with a cool one of his own.

'Then you in luck, boy,' said Shiv.

'Why's that?'

'Cos things about to kick off on Coronation Road.' Shiv took a couple of steps forward, his shiny leather coat flapping at his heels. He had a weird smile on his face that made him seem scarier than ever. I wondered for a second what he'd done to get his name. 'You see da news, right?'

'I heard some guy got beaten up,' said Tokes, standing his ground with a shrug.

'That's my cuz you talkin' about,' Shiv snapped. 'Show some respect!'

'Yeah, Pats, he like a 'sleb now!' said Pea excitedly. 'He on da front page of every newspaper and on da news too!'

I thought of the footage I had of my mum telling me to steer clear of boys like that.

'So you hear it was da police who put him in hospital?' asked Shiv.

'I heard that was the rumour,' said Tokes.

'More than a rumour. We got a witness, innit,' said Shiv, glancing at Pea.

Tokes raised his eyebrows. 'A reliable one?' he said, also flicking his eyes in Pea's direction.

Shiv laughed and patted Little Pea on the head. 'He sweared on his mamma's life!'

Pea did a little jig, a broad grin breaking out on his face. 'It be mega dope, man!' he chirruped as Tokes shook his head in disbelief. 'There gonna be a riot! Coronation Road goin' down in flames.'

'Ain't that the truth,' said Shiv. 'The police gonna pay for what they done to my cuz. An' that is why this yo lucky day, boy.'

Tokes screwed up his face, like something tasted bad. 'Oh yeah?'

Shiv smiled and narrowed his snake eyes. 'Look, North

London boy. Da way I sees it you got two choices.'

'Really?' Tokes blinked hard as if the light was hurting his eyes. That was when I wondered if he was more scared than he was making out.

'Cos no one pushes Shiv round like you done and gets to live. You get that, right?'

Tad made a spitting noise in the back of his throat, like a camel. I must have had the camera facing right at them at that point, because on the film you can just see the corner of Tad's pale freckly face on the screen. Shiv's eyes fill the rest of the lens.

'If you say so,' said Tokes coolly.

'I do.' Shiv paused. 'But you new round here. Don't know what's what,' he went on, glancing warningly at Tad. 'An' if they gonna be war 'gainst the police in this hood, we need as many foot soldiers as we can get. You hearin' me?'

Tokes looked around him, taking in the piles of litter in the gutters and the rusty railings in front of the youth club, and Shiv's two bodyguards, both ready to pull him apart at the first sign from Shiv. Tokes was acting like he wasn't frightened though and I think that's why Shiv wanted him so bad.

'So what do you want me to do?' said Tokes slowly.

'Come an' join da Starfish Gang,' said Shiv.

Little Pea did a skip and a hop and squeaked, 'Told you I got you a job interview, dittn't I, North London boy!'

Tokes didn't even look at him. He just closed his eyes and let out a long, low whistle between his teeth. 'And what if I say no?'

'Then we got plenty ways of makin' you regret it,' said Shiv, his voice taut with casual menace.

'I'm not afraid of you,' Tokes responded quietly.

Shiv laughed. 'I'm not talkin' 'bout broken bones, boy,' he said with a weird little smile flickering on his lips. 'Mebbe I ask Detective Pea here to track down yo daddy,' Shiv said quietly. 'Tell him we find his long-lost son, right?'

Tokes's eyes were paler than usual and his fingers were balled into fists at his side. 'Whatever,' he said, his jaw still tight. 'You'd never find my dad anyway.'

'No?' said Shiv, glancing at Pea who was grinning like a maniac. 'How you know we ain't already got his number on speed dial?'

There was a second's pause and then Tokes launched himself at Shiv – all cool suddenly gone. In a flash, he was shoving Shiv backwards, yelling, 'Just leave my dad out of this!'

But Shiv was laughing, not fighting back at all, and it was Little Pea who put a hand on Tokes's chest and said, 'Easy, bro.'

'I ain't your brother, you hear me!' Tokes yelled. He backed up, panting, his eyes darting from Pea to Shiv, his whole body shaking with anger. 'Just quit messing with my family, OK?'

'You unnerstand,' Shiv went on. 'You know how it rolls, dontcha, boy? You either with us or you against us.'

Tokes kept staring at his feet and shaking his head. 'I heard that one before, and I'm not buying it. Not this time.'

When I look back at the stuff I filmed that day (lots of it wobbly and out of focus), I find myself wondering what would have happened if he'd said yes. Whether things would have turned out differently. Whether nobody would have died or had to disappear.

But he just shook his head at Pea – gutted now, no longer angry – and said, 'You really set this up?'

Pea was skipping again like the ground was red-hot. 'I done you a favour, North London boy, an' you crazy if you turn it down.'

'Da Pea's right. I offerin' you a chance here, boy,' said Shiv. 'There gonna be fires ragin' all over this hood. You gonna run with us or burn with da rest?'

There was a long pause. From the station above an announcement declared that services were delayed due to soaring temperatures buckling the rails.

Then Tokes looked up and said quietly, 'Thanks for the offer, but no thanks.'

'Say what, boy?' said Tad in a stupid gangsta-rap voice.

'I've got enough friends already,' said Tokes, tipping his head in my direction. 'I don't need no more.'

'The posh kid?' Tad laughed, his strawberry-lace legs wobbling like strings. 'You choosin' some white girl over a chance to run with da Starfish Gang?'

'Yes,' said Tokes with an odd smile on his face. 'Looks like I am.' Then he turned to me, stuck out his hand and said, 'You coming, Maggie?'

He was staring at me and I glanced from him to Shiv to Pea and back again, my face suddenly aflame and my legs refusing to move.

'Um – yeah,' I stammered.

Pea giggled nervously. He was looking frightened, I thought. Tad let out a long, low whistle as I took Tokes's hand and let him tug me in the direction of the exit.

But Shiv wasn't letting us go that easily. 'Hey, North of da River,' he called after us.

Tokes stopped, but he didn't turn round.

'You not know when it gonna happen, not know how it gonna happen, but for sure we gon' take you out, boy,' Shiv said slowly, low-voiced but seriously full of threat.

Tokes still didn't turn round. His hand in mine felt hot and sweaty, but he just shrugged and said, 'I'll look forward to it.'

SCENE 12: CORONATION ROAD

It was hard to keep pace because Tokes was walking so quickly, like he was worried we were being followed. He headed straight towards Coronation Road and I trotted after him.

'Where are we going?' I asked, panting as I tried to keep up.

'Somewhere really busy where there's loads of people and CCTV,' he said without even looking at me. Glancing at him, I could see he was sweating and that his eyes were suddenly very bright.

'Why?'

He turned and gave me a sort of grin. 'We need to go somewhere Shiv can't beat me to a pulp. That's why!'

'Oh,' I said. 'Yeah – makes sense.'

'Come on then.'

So we emerged on to Coronation Road and almost immediately we were lost in the hustle and bustle and Tokes let go of my hand, but didn't slow down. We kept walking, past the stalls selling pirate DVDs and giant suitcases, past the pound shops and the Caribbean general store, past the most held-up post office in London and the pub with the boarded-up windows where the Richardson Gang used to plot their turf war against the Krays.

Tokes only slowed down as we approached the electrical store. The TV screens in the window were showing more footage from the arrests the other night. It was blurry, taken on somebody's mobile phone: dark hooded figures under the street lamps, policemen bearing down on them with batons, shoving them into police vans. The headline on one read: *Protestors gather outside police station as minister denies rumours of police brutality*.

Tokes stopped for a second and I pulled out my camera and filmed the six TVs all showing the same pictures. I filmed Tokes staring at them. I could still feel the imprint of his hand on mine. He looked up and caught my eye, but I blushed and turned away.

Ishmael Choudhary was behind the counter, talking to a customer about a phone. He caught sight of me, nodded and smiled. I was suddenly incredibly conscious of Tokes standing next to me. I raised my hand in quick greeting then turned away, aware that I was blushing more madly than ever.

Tokes stared for a second at Ishmael then turned back to me with a puzzled expression on his face. 'Who's that?' he asked.

'No one,' I said quickly. 'Just a friend.'

'Oh,' he said.

I could feel him looking at me still and suddenly everything felt weird between us, so I said, 'We should get out of here. Go somewhere Shiv will never look for us. I know somewhere.'

'OK.' He reached out and took my hand again and I felt like a little electric shock had run through my fingers. 'Come on.'

We kept moving, past the off-licence with its bulletproof glass and the jerk chicken shop and the Marry-Me bridal store, which is where Tokes turned to me and said, 'You know, you'd probably be safer if you didn't hang out with me.'

'I know,' I said, dropping my eyes.

'So, um, you should go home. Stay out of this.'

He'd let go of my hand, but I could still feel his fingers on my palm, even hotter than they'd been before, as he looked at me with anxious eyes.

I shook my head, not wanting to leave him. 'You said we were in this together.'

'Seriously, Maggie, I'm bad news.' Tokes's grey-brown eyes clouded as he spoke. 'A magnet for trouble. No matter how hard I try to stay clear, it follows me everywhere.'

'A bit like me then?' I said, looking up and meeting his eyes with a nervous smile. 'Following you everywhere, I mean.'

He grinned, but his eyes still looked sad. 'I'm just saying I won't mind if you want to cut out.'

'I don't want to,' I said.

'OK, but if I tell you to go it's for your own good, right – and you've got to do what I say, OK?'

I nodded and said, 'OK.' But I knew even then that I didn't really mean it. That I couldn't leave him now, even if I wanted to.

It was my idea to go to the picture gallery because I figured it was the last place the Starfish Gang would come looking for us. Shiv and Tad didn't exactly strike me as the cultured types. So, after Tokes had given up trying to persuade me to go home, I led him through the backstreets and round the twisty rows of terraces till we reached the leafier lanes where most of the rich people live.

It felt like another world to the one we'd left behind. As soon as you cross the line from Coronation Road to the upmarket borough where me and my mum live, little delis and boutiques start to appear, their sparkling windows full of beautiful, useless stuff. People dress differently and even the sun seems to shine more softly and golden, richer.

The best thing is that we're invisible here. If I was on my own, it would be different, but because we don't fit we walk like ghosts through the posh streets. You'd think it would be the opposite, but it's not. My mum says that's what class means: people not being able to see each other. It's the parallel universes thing again. Maybe she has a point.

We walked in silence for ages, but, as we went past a massive posh school, Tokes asked, 'Is that like your school?'

I think maybe he wanted to talk about other stuff to take his mind off what had just happened, so I said, 'Sort of. Only, um, I go to a boarding school.'

'Cool!' he said, nodding even though he looked as if his thoughts were miles away. 'So what's that like then?'

'I hate it,' I said, staring down at my boots.

'Why?' He turned to look at me properly then.

I hesitated, trying to explain stuff I spent most of the time trying not to think about. 'When you've got a mum like mine, everyone expects a lot of you. I guess I'm always a disappointment.'

'What about friends? Boyfriends?'

I pulled at a bit of my purple fringe to avoid meeting his eye. 'I've never been very good at stuff like that,' I said. I didn't say that I'd got worse since Mum and Dad split up because I had a feeling he already knew that.

'Well, you've got me now,' said Tokes. 'Most wanted boy in Coronation Road. What more can you ask for?'

He laughed then, a funny dry laugh like autumn leaves, and it made me laugh too. An old lady walking past gave us a strange look and that made us laugh even more.

'What about you?' I said, after we'd walked a bit more. 'Do you like school?'

'Yeah,' he said. 'I do. But I guess I'm the opposite of you. No one expects anything good of someone like me.'

'Why?'

He shrugged. 'Teachers see where you come from and they just expect you to drop out, mess up, go off the rails.'

'But you're clever,' I said. 'They must have realised that.'

'Some teachers just see what they want to,' he said with another shrug. And I found myself thinking that maybe all schools were sort of the same in that way.

'Miss Kayacan, my English teacher, she was different,' he went on. 'I mean, she was young and cool and –' He hesitated then added quickly, 'Sort of pretty. But that wasn't why I liked her. She – I dunno.' He frowned. 'She believed in me, I guess. Told me I had the potential to do well. Go to university if I wanted. She saw the best in me, like my mum does. And it makes a difference, you know, when someone believes in you.'

I nodded, thinking of the way my mum looked at me sometimes – like she worried about me, felt sorry for me, expected me every moment to fall apart, never that she believed in me.

'So that's why you turned Shiv down?'

'I'm not gonna let my mum down,' he said firmly.

'Cos you do know if you were in the Starfish Gang you'd be safe,' I said. 'Nobody could touch you.'

He shook his head. 'No way, Maggie. Being in a gang doesn't make you safe. Look at Little Pea. Or my dad.' He tailed off as he mentioned his dad.

'But now you're gang enemy number one,' I said. 'Isn't that worse?'

Tokes turned his face to me and he looked like he'd seen stuff that had made him grow up way too fast. 'Maybe,' he said. 'But at least I've chosen what side I'm on. I'd rather go down in flames with you than rule the streets with someone like Shiv.'

'Hey, peeps! Where you goin'?' a voice called out from behind us. I looked back and there was Little Pea, running after us, his arms and legs flailing, his pea-shaped face lit up with a giant clown-like grin.

'Seriously?' said Tokes, shaking his head in disbelief. 'I don't *believe* this kid!'

Pea screeched to a halt, puffing and panting like mad. 'Wait up!'

'Are you actually stalking us now?' said Tokes.

'Look, Shiv's even madder at me than ever, man,' Pea puffed. 'An' it all cos of you!'

'*I'm* mad at you!' said Tokes, kicking at the pavement.

'What for?' Pea squeaked, his face a picture of genuine

astonishment. 'I did you a serious favour back there.'

'No, you didn't,' said Tokes. 'Didn't it even cross your mind I might not say yes to him?'

Pea shrugged. 'No, cos I thinked you got more sense than that. Be-sides,' he grinned and did another little shimmy, 'I figured either way it be a good bit of drama for our movie.' Pea did another skip when he said that and grinned broadly.

Tokes shook his head. 'What do you want, Pea?'

'Oh, I gotta bring you a message. From Shiv.'

'Go on then.'

'He say you a dead man walkin',' Pea said bluntly.

'Right,' said Tokes wearily. 'Anything else?'

Little Pea skipped on the hot tarmac and grinned in my direction. 'You wanna film this, Hollywood?' he asked me. 'Cos this is one of them life-changin' decision moments. You know, when your hero – that's me – is faced with an impossible choice, a choice that will affect da lives of all da other characters in da story. Gotta get it on film, I thinkin'!'

I glanced at Tokes who just shrugged.

'Um – yeah, I suppose.' I flicked my camera out of the pouch round my neck and turned it to focus on the twitchy, grinning Pea who seemed totally out of place here in the posh part of town.

'You rollin'?' he asked, staring at the camera.

I nodded. 'Lights, camera, action . . .'

It's actually quite funny when you watch it back. Because Pea put on this pained, tragic TV face and milked his moment for all it was worth.

'So here's da deal. Shiv say you both on da Wanted list now an' . . .' His face was solemn but with a naughty twinkle in his eye. 'An' I gotta be da one to bring you down.'

'Right. So what you gonna do?' asked Tokes calmly. 'Stab us in the back – again? Push us under a bus? Slip us a poison pill? Or you gonna take your chances with Shiv?'

'Not sure yet,' grinned Pea, breaking out of his film-star face suddenly. 'I thought I'd hang wit' you peeps for a bit then decide if I gonna take you down or join your gang.'

'Did we ever actually *invite* you to join our gang?' said Tokes.

'Hey! You know you wanna be frien's with da Pea!' he squeaked, looking crestfallen but hopeful at the same time. 'See, I figure you, Mr Tokes, can't resist a lost cause, and Miss Hollywood there can see I got on-screen potential. So it only a matter of time before we all bessies.'

He smiled like he was in some kind of beauty pageant and Tokes sighed.

'An' you either be my frien's for da day or I goin' off on a Daddy hunt north of da river,' Pea added cheerfully. 'What's it gonna be?'

*

So all three of us went to the gallery to check out the old pictures in massive gold frames. I used to go there sometimes on my own in the holidays because you can sit for ages in the cool, dim interior and nobody bothers you. It's quiet at midday – hardly anyone looking round. And I like the pictures, the way they say stuff with light and shade and colour.

'This stuff is well old,' said Pea, staring at the paintings of knights and ladies and people going hunting on horses with loads of little dogs running round their feet.

Tokes was gazing around with wide eyes. He seemed lost in thought. He'd hardly said a word since Pea attached himself to us, like a ticking, non-stop-talking time bomb.

'Hey! I got an idea!' Pea was saying, his eyes twinkling, his wide white smile bright in the gloom. 'We should do one of dem montage t'ings. You know, like in da movies when they try on loads of outfits and pull kooky faces.'

'We can't,' I said, glancing round at the gallery attendant who was already glaring in our direction.

'Come on, Hollywood, sometimes you gotta take risks for your art,' Pea grinned. 'You just hold da camera. I'll do da rest.'

The next thing I knew Pea was skidding round the museum, posing in front of different pictures, pulling sad faces, silly faces, thoughtful faces, and I had to film him. Sometimes he jumped in the air, other times he got down and sort of knee-walked in front of them. When we got to the portraits, he imitated each sitter, from sober old women to knights wielding swords, to beautiful dead ladies floating in weeds and little cherubs frolicking naked on clouds.

We had to keep dodging the gallery attendant, but Pea had years of practice hiding from people so he had a sixth sense about when he was coming.

'Come on!' he said as he dragged me round another corner just as the attendant appeared from the opposite entrance.

'How do you do that?' I said, peering back into the room we'd just left where the attendant stood, looking around with a puzzled expression on his face.

'Da devil in me bones gives me X-ray vision, innit,' said Pea proudly. 'I see t'ings ordinary peeps don't.'

'Like what happened to Shiv's cousin?' Tokes said, looking up suddenly. He'd been lagging behind, not saying anything, like he was trying to figure something out.

'Wouldn't you like to know!' said Pea who had started posing under the picture of a naked cherub, pouting just like the blond, blue-eyed babe. He sort of carried it off weirdly. Then he jumped out of the pose. 'But it your turn to take da stage now so that info gonna have to wait.'

'What?' I said.

'It only a montage if we *all* do it.' Pea grinned mischievously.

'Now I get to hold da camera, while you an' North of da River pose.'

Tokes was staring hard at Little Pea. 'Why are you doing this?' he asked.

'Um, cos it be well cool,' giggled Pea.

'Not the montage. I mean, why are you hanging with the Starfish? Taking your orders from someone like Shiv?'

I was expecting Pea to come back with a retort right away, but he didn't. He twitched and his eyes took on a nervous, suspicious look.

'Because you know they're only using you, right?' Tokes went on. 'Shiv will drop you the moment you're no use to them any more.'

'Ack, I be dead long before then.' Little Pea shrugged, trying to sound matter-of-fact about it. 'Don't you know, kids like me always da first casualties in gang warfare.'

Tokes kept looking at him and a shadow crossed over his face. 'It doesn't have to be like that,' he said.

Pea was still grinning, but his brow was puckered and his toes were twitching up and down like this conversation made him more nervous than Shiv's knife against his neck. 'Youngers like me don't got a choice,' he said. 'Dontcha know that by now?'

'Everyone's got choices,' said Tokes simply.

'Not me. I an abused child, mister,' said Pea, still with the same flickering, hunted look in his eyes. 'Victim of urban poverty. No point fighting fate, issit? You'll see. It da same for you too. You can take da boy outta da gang, but you can't take da gang outta da boy.'

He stared at Tokes with a hint of a challenge in his eyes when he said that. Tokes just shook his head, but he didn't reply.

'So,' said Pea, brighter than ever, 'you gonna be part of this montage or not?'

Tokes sighed. 'Fine, but you've got to promise me something.'

'What?'

'If you decide you don't want to be pushed around by the Starfish any more . . .'

'I won't!' Pea declared.

'OK, but if you do, you come and hang with us, OK?'

Pea looked at him curiously, his eyes narrowed. I remembered what Tokes had said about him not trusting people who were nice to him. 'Why?'

'Why what?'

'Why you bein' nice to me when all I bring you is trouble?'

Tokes hesitated. 'Cos it doesn't seem like you've got anyone else.'

'Hey, I got plenty of people, me,' said Pea quickly, but he didn't sound convincing. He looked from me to Tokes, rolled his eyes in imitation of Tokes then said, 'You ask me, you gotta hero complex. Path-o-log-ical need to go round savin' peeps from danger.'

'Maybe, but that's better than having a self-destruct button that takes out everyone you ever talk to,' Tokes replied.

'Gonna get you killed a lot quicker though,' said Pea with a cheeky little wiggle. 'So,' he grinned. 'Montage time.'

Pea filmed while me and Tokes did some daft stuff together. He kept yelling out directions like we were on a fashion shoot: 'Vogue it! Now pout. Give me a lion face. More. More. Make love to da camera.' And after a bit we were all laughing and we seemed to have forgotten about the giant, Shiv-shaped shadow hanging over us.

The museum was pretty empty and we'd managed to get away from the man on duty, but I could see an elderly couple in the gallery next door. I reckon Pea could see them too as he came to a panting halt in front of a picture of some people at a fancy ball and declared loudly, 'You gotta dance now. You know, like the stuff they do on that *Strictly* dancing show.'

'What . . . no . . .!'

Tokes was shaking his head and I was protesting, but Pea didn't listen. He pushed me and Tokes together, grabbing his arms and wrapping them round my waist. 'You jus' hold her like this and she put her hands up here like this –'

My heart leapt as if I'd had an electric shock as Tokes's hands touched my waist. Tokes was trying to pull away, but Pea wouldn't let him.

'Then you just gotta twirl around a bit – mebbe you tip her back or spin her under your arm, you know,' Pea went on, now talking with an accent like he was some foreign dance coach.

'This is stupid,' said Tokes, not looking me in the eye. I could feel myself blushing madly. My face was right up against his chest and I could feel the heat of his skin, smell the toothpaste and cold chips and the scent of his body, hear his heart pounding under his thin T-shirt.

'You do da moves, I do da music!' said Pea, jumping up on a bench and starting to do some 'boom-chaka' thingy, his head wobbling up and down like a rag doll's as he rapped out the beat. 'Twirl!' he commanded.

I stared hard at my thin white hands next to the dark brown of the skin on Tokes's neck. I could hear my own heartbeat and my breath coming fast.

'You meant to look like you totally in love an' stuff!' commanded Pea, breaking off his music again. 'Come on, romance it up a bit, right.'

I felt Tokes glance at me and then look quickly away again. Beneath the thin cotton of his T-shirt I could feel his heart was beating faster than usual too and the skin on his neck was flushed.

'Fine,' he said tightly. 'But this is totally the last thing. Then I'm done, you understand?'

'Sure, man!' Little Pea's beatbox got louder and louder and he started dancing along with jerky movements which made him look like he was having a fit. Somehow he managed to keep filming at the same time. 'Now I wanna see some dirty dancin' from you twose!'

Tokes's fingers on my waist felt like electrodes as we attempted a shaky twirl. It was the same as when Ishmael looked at me, only worse somehow: more painful, more acute. My face burned so hot I thought it must be the colour of my boots, and my heart was beating so hard it hurt in my brain.

Pea was grinning widely. 'Love is in da air!' he sang.

'Stop it!' muttered Tokes.

'If you say so,' sing-songed Pea.

That was when the old couple appeared in the doorway. I remember the surprised expressions in their eyes.

I stumbled over my feet and crashed into Tokes. 'I'm sorry, I . . .'

Tokes took a quick step back, Pea ground to a stuttering halt and we all stood, staring at the grey-haired lady and the bald old man who were frozen in the doorway.

'It's a wrap!' giggled Pea.

SCENE 13: OUTSIDE THE PICTURE GALLERY

'What I tell you?' said Pea, flopping down on to the grass in the park. 'Was that good or what?'

The sun was shining more fiercely than ever and it seemed unbearably hot after the cool of the gallery, especially since I was still burning with embarrassment.

'We should find some music an' play it in da background. It be well funny!' Pea was saying, breathless from running and excitement.

'We?' said Tokes, raising an eyebrow as he stretched himself out full length on the ground next to where I was sitting, not looking at me.

'You gotta let me in on da film now!' wailed Pea. 'I a creative genius, innit! So where we gonna go next?'

He looked at me with expectant eyes and I still couldn't work out if he really wanted to help or if this was just another one of his tricks.

I glanced quickly at Tokes who had his hands under his head and was staring up at the sky. He looked taller when he was laid out flat and his T-shirt rode up, revealing the flat, dark skin of his belly.

'So does that mean you're gonna tell Shiv where to stick it?' Tokes was asking.

'Aw! Come on, man!' Pea pleaded. 'You know I can't do that. I be on my best behaviour though! Promise!' He pulled a wide-eyed, pleading face, but Tokes just rolled his eyes.

I shifted my eyes away from Tokes's tummy, pulled my legs up under my chin and wrapped my arms round my knees. I was still conscious of the imprint of Tokes's fingers on the small of my back.

'Like I said, if you want to go straight then you can hang with us. Otherwise . . .' Tokes tailed off, shrugging.

Pea scowled and went all twitchy again, refusing to look at either of us for a moment. Then he jerked his phone out of his pocket and flipped it open even though we hadn't heard it ring. 'Sure. Yeah,' he yelled into it way too loud. 'Yeah, I comin' right back, Mamma.'

He put the phone down and looked at us with a weird expression on his face. 'Dat was my mamma.'

'I never heard your phone ring,' said Tokes.

'It on a special vibrate,' said Pea, his eyes darting testily from side to side. 'Anyways, I gotta split,' he said, blinking rapidly. 'Been nice hangin' wit' you – and da pictures.' He giggled. 'Mebbe we do it again sometime.'

'Maybe,' said Tokes, sitting up now to look at him curiously.

But Pea had already started off in the direction of the road, moving like the ground was as hot as coals and burning his feet as he skipped backwards.

'Cool dance moves,' he yelled out as he went. 'An' you sure make a lovely couple!'

Colour shot back into my cheeks and neither of us said anything for a minute.

'What did I tell you?' said Tokes at last. He shook his head, but his eyes avoided mine. 'That kid changes sides more often than a tennis ball.'

I nodded, shoving my hands in my pockets and staring at the ground.

That was when I realised.

'Hey,' I exclaimed. 'My camera. Pea's taken it!'

SCENE 14: MAGGIE'S BEDROOM

My bedroom is the only room in our house where I don't feel like I'm in the way. I decorated it myself. Just after my dad left I went out and got a tin of black chalkboard paint. When my mum came home from work, I'd already painted two of the walls. I thought she'd go mad, but she just shook her head and said if I wanted to live in a tomb then that was my choice.

She made me leave the other two walls white, but she lets me doodle all over the chalkboard paint. I've done cartoons of people, animals, smiley faces, whatever really, and then there are lines from my favourite films, and stuff I've overheard while I'm undercover – cool, mad stuff people say when they think no one is listening.

The white walls are covered with posters and stills from my favourite movies – from *ET* to *Scott Pilgrim*, *The Breakfast Club* to *Donnie Darko*. And there are some storyboards I've sketched too. Some of them are in pencil and ink right on to the wall (I sort of hoped Mum'd go mad about that too, but she doesn't even have time to get angry any more); others are on long strips of paper hanging on string from the ceiling.

As Tokes stared around at it all, it felt a bit like he was looking inside my head. Maybe that's why I didn't bring him up here last time he came over.

'I like it,' he said. 'It's not like the rest of the house, is it?'

'That's the point,' I said.

He was looking at the doodles and the posters. His face was still creased into a frown, and he seemed distracted, like he was still thinking about Little Pea and the camera. 'It looks like you,' he said.

He might have smiled at me when he said that, but I'm not sure because I looked away.

'What music do you think we should use for the montage?' I said quickly, flicking on my laptop, awkward suddenly. All the footage I'd taken that morning appeared right away, just like Ishmael had said it would.

'Haven't we lost it all? I mean, if Pea's got the camera, that is.'

I'd been trying not to think about Pea having my camera, or about what would happen if he showed it to Shiv, because whenever I did I felt a jolt of fear in my stomach that I couldn't quite dislodge afterwards.

'Oh, it syncs automatically with my laptop,' I said, turning back to look at him. 'The stuff we filmed today will be on here already.'

'Right,' he said. He still sounded distracted somehow. 'How did you manage that?'

'Ish–' I stopped, colouring. 'My friend from the electrical store did it for me,' I said awkwardly.

Tokes looked up then and gave me a look I couldn't quite make out. 'The young guy? Is he a friend of yours?'

'No – yes – I mean . . .' I stammered, blushing furiously. 'I know his dad. A bit.'

'Right.' Tokes shrugged like it was no big deal, but he still had a weird expression on his face. 'Well, that's cool then, I suppose.'

'Yeah,' I said. Then my heart sank again as I remembered the bigger problem. 'Except if Pea decides to show the stuff we filmed to Shiv.'

Tokes sighed and frowned again, but he said, 'I don't think he will. Not yet anyway.'

'Why not?' I looked at him hopefully.

'Because then he wouldn't have anything over us,' said Tokes simply, although I wasn't sure if he really believed what he was saying.

'Really?' I said, my stomach twisting with a mixture of anxiety and hope.

'Oh, who the hell knows with that kid!' Tokes's smile didn't quite reach his eyes. Then he shrugged and said, 'But let's stop thinking about Pea for a bit. Haven't we got a movie to make?'

So that's what we did. And somehow it worked and I stopped feeling anxious for a while. I sat on the bed and Tokes sat cross-legged on the floor, and we both munched doughnuts and watched every single thing I'd filmed that summer and laughed and talked and made plans for the movie. There was stuff I'd shot before we met: random things like shop signs; the map outside Coronation Road Station; a duvet cover on a market stall that read Home Sweet Home; Mr Choudhary waving to me from behind the counter of Choudhary's Electrical Store. Even the images of Ishmael.

Most of it was silent – just random pictures with no story. The action didn't really start until the confrontation in the park when Little Pea appeared on-screen, face looming round and manic, close to the camera. The camera angle drew your eye to the scars on his head and his cheeks. Even his crazy voice and his twitchy body seemed magnified on-screen.

'Natural-born film star,' Tokes observed. 'Just like he said.'

Then we got to the bit with my mum.

'Oh, this is nothing,' I said, skipping quickly through the footage. It was blurry and badly lit, but her face was visible – her eyes staring hard at me even on fast forward. I don't know why, but for some reason I didn't want him to see her looking so beautiful or maybe I didn't want him to think badly of her. I don't know. But he didn't ask and so I didn't have to try to explain.

Then we watched back the showdown this morning. The audio was a bit fuzzy and lots of the shots were of the wall or the arches. Occasionally, I'd caught Tokes and Shiv on-screen, heads cut off, blurry and unfocused, or a moment of Little Pea's feet dancing on the hot gravel. You could still feel the menace though. I glanced at Tokes as we watched it and saw that his face was pale and his jaw was set in something like concentration.

Finally, there was the montage in the art gallery, which was actually really funny. Pea had managed to catch the expression on the old lady's face when she walked in and found him beatboxing in front of a priceless oil painting. And there was a shot of Tokes with his arms round me, a close-up on both our faces which made my heart go bump and which seemed to last forever on the film.

'What do you think?' I said quickly when it came to an end.

Tokes nodded. 'I think it could be cool.'

'You reckon?'

'Yeah.' He grinned. 'You shot some great stuff. And it's kind of got a story already, hasn't it?'

'It hasn't really got an ending though.'

'I guess that'll come when it's ready. And I've got loads of ideas already for what we can do with this lot,' he said enthusiastically. Then he hesitated. 'If you're OK with it, that is?'

I nodded, caught up in his sunshine smile, excited suddenly.

'Come on then,' he said. 'Let's get this film rolling!'

So we spent ages cutting and editing and moving stuff round like a collage, making a story out of the pictures. Then we went on YouTube to find bits of music for the montage, messing around with it to make it fit. Working on the film with Tokes felt so different to doing it on my own. His words and my pictures seemed to fit together and make each other sparkle.

After a bit Petra stuck her head round the door and shattered the mood. 'Your mother called,' she said, her sleepy eyes blinking.

I looked up, shy suddenly. I'd slid off the mattress and Tokes and I were now sitting side by side, leaning against the bed, the laptop on the floor between us.

'What did she want?' I asked crossly.

'She say tell you to keep away from Coronation Road and specially police station,' said Petra in a bored-sounding voice. 'She say there trouble down there.'

I quickly glanced at Tokes then away again. 'Anything else?'

'She say she be back late. Eat without her.'

'Of course,' I said. 'Now please can you leave us alone? We're kind of busy here.'

Petra took one more look at Tokes, sniffed then disappeared.

There was a moment's silence after she'd gone and I was conscious of how close we were. I shifted a little so that there was a bit more of a gap between us.

'What do you think she meant – trouble at the police station?' Tokes asked eventually.

'Maybe it's something to do with Pats,' I said. 'We should probably check it out.' I flicked on the TV until I found the twenty-four-hour news channel. It was showing images of the police station down the end of Coronation Road. I recognised the old Victorian frontage.

'She's right,' muttered Tokes. 'Something's going on.'

The footage showed a crowd – there must have been fifty or maybe even a hundred people milling round the steps and spilling out along the pavement and the road, holding up the traffic. Some of them had placards saying stuff like 'Justice for Pats Karunga' and 'Action on Police Brutality', and there was a lot of shouting and shaking of fists.

The announcer was saying, 'The police have issued a statement denying all responsibility for the injuries sustained by Patrick Karunga, who is still in a critical condition in hospital.'

Tokes let out a long whistling breath.

'Meanwhile, a witness has come forward, claiming to have seen two officers brutally assaulting Mr Karunga.'

'Do you think that's Pea?' I said.

Tokes shrugged. 'I wouldn't be surprised.'

Suddenly my mum appeared on the screen and I felt my stomach lurch. She was wearing the same suit she had on in the Tony Blair picture, with bright red lipstick. She looked as beautiful as ever and I could see Tokes's eyes widen as he stared at her. For some reason that made me hate her even more.

'As tensions continue to grow in Coronation Road, local MP Harriet Hatton called for crowds to go home and let the police do their job,' said the announcer.

'Isn't that your mum?' said Tokes, turning to me. I nodded glumly.

She looked smaller on-screen – even with her mega-heels on – but she seemed to glow as she said, 'Rumours of police brutality are completely untrue.'

'Not according to Pea,' I muttered.

'Patrick Karunga is a known gang member with a history of drug-dealing and violent confrontations with other gangs,' Mum went on calmly and insistently, her face a perfect mask. 'The police have my full support.'

The picture flicked to the next news story then and I muted it before flopping back on to the bed.

'She makes it sound like it was Pats's fault,' said Tokes.

I nodded. 'She's good at that. Do you reckon Pea really saw what happened?'

'Who knows. I don't know what to believe with that kid.'

'But why would he make it up?'

'Maybe Shiv told him to. Maybe he's protecting somebody. Maybe he thought it'd be fun.' He stopped and stared at the blank TV screen, his face scrunched up in thought. 'Or maybe he's frightened of something.'

'You think Pea's in trouble?'

'I think he's probably more scared of Shiv than he is of the police.'

'Why would he be scared of the police?'

Tokes turned and looked at me disbelievingly for a second. Then he stretched out his hand and stared down at it. He had long slender fingers with neatly cut nails. 'Have you ever been stop-and-searched?' he asked quietly.

I shook my head.

'Well, you can bet Pea has,' he said, running his fingers over the soft cream of the carpet. 'And, once that's happened to you, the police don't seem so much like heroes any more.'

I hesitated before asking, 'Has it happened to you?'

Tokes was staring straight down, the sun on his face making his eyes look paler than usual. His palm was spread out like a starfish on the carpet.

'The first time, I was ten years old,' he said. 'My mum sent me out for some milk at the local shop and this police car pulled up. They even put cuffs on me.'

'Handcuffs?'

He nodded and I noticed that his starfish hand was now balled into a fist. I wanted to reach out and touch it, but I didn't.

'Was that the only time?' I asked.

'No, that was just the first,' he said. 'I guess I just look the type, you know?'

He shrugged and looked up at me, his face clearing as he said, 'Told you I was a magnet for trouble, didn't I? Anyway, what I'm saying is, plenty of kids like Pea have got reason to hate or fear the police already. It only takes a little spark to start a fire.'

I looked at the chalk drawings all over the wall – silly doodles, white swirls against the black paint – and I knew I should say something, but I couldn't think what. It felt suddenly as if we were worlds apart. In parallel universes, side by side, but never actually touching.

'If it all kicks off, that's bad for your mum, right?' Tokes said after a moment.

I nodded. 'Probably.'

'She should promise an inquiry then,' said Tokes. 'Because the way she's talking at the moment makes it sound like a cover-up.'

I looked at Tokes and I wondered what my mum would think about taking political advice from a boy like him. The idea made me smile for some reason. He smiled too and we were in the same universe again.

Then suddenly my phone rang. Tokes picked it up and tossed it to me.

I glanced at the screen and saw Little Pea's face grinning up at me: 'The Pea-man' said the caller ID. I clicked answer.

'Pea? How the hell did you get your photo on my phone?'

I heard his squeaky voice on the other end of the line. It sounded tinny and desperate. Then I turned to Tokes and said, 'It's Pea. He's hurt.'

SCENE 15: MAGGIE'S DEN

Pea was behind the squat house, lying on the sofa. His face was covered in blood and one of his eyes was so badly swollen it wouldn't even open. I'd never in my life seen anyone properly beaten up like that – only in films – and I gasped in shock because it's so much worse in real life.

'Who did this to you?' Tokes asked fiercely.

Pea just shook his head. 'Camera,' he muttered and from his pocket he pulled it out.

'Surprise, surprise!' Tokes said. 'We knew you'd nicked it.'

'Borrowed it!'

'And what exactly did you do with it?' Tokes said.

'Wouldn't you like to know!' Pea grinned then grimaced.

'Did you show it to Shiv?' I asked.

I'd switched on the camera and was flicking quickly through the footage from the last couple of days. 'Nothing's been deleted,' I said. 'Did you watch all the stuff on here?' I asked Pea, although I already knew the answer.

'Look, are you gonna film this or what?' said Pea grumpily. 'I'm ain't sayin' nuttin' till you press record. An' neither of you seems too concerned that I bleedin' here, issit?'

Tokes rolled his eyes, but I could tell he was worried. 'You need to let me clean you up,' he said. We'd swiped the first-aid kit from my kitchen and Tokes was brandishing a packet of antiseptic wipes. 'Those cuts look bad.'

'Just be sure to leave some blood on my face,' Pea said, wriggling as Tokes dabbed at the blood below his ear. 'That look good on film, innit. All da girls love a hard man.'

'Proper little drama queen, aren't you?' said Tokes.

'You bet!' said Pea with a crooked smile. 'Now get da film rollin'.'

I sighed and pressed record.

I read an article once about special effects, like fake blood and wounds. It was all about prosthetic putty and stuff like that, but also about camera angles and how to make wounds 'tell a story'. I kept thinking about that as I was filming – what Pea's injuries were telling us about what had happened to him. But all I could really see was that someone had hurt him badly.

'OK, now talk,' Tokes demanded as Pea winced and twitched at the touch of the antiseptic wipes. 'Who did this to you? Was it Shiv?'

'Ow! That hurt, man,' said Pea, shivering like a baby. 'An'

I cold too, innit. Mebbe I sufferin' from shock. You got a jacket on you?'

Tokes tugged a hoodie out of his rucksack and threw it at Pea who grinned and wrapped it round his shoulders like an old lady in a shawl. It was too big for him and he looked lost within it; his head balanced on top like a tiny little marble, all covered in cuts and bruises.

'So was it Shiv?' Tokes asked again.

Pea shrugged.

'Why did he do it?' I asked, focusing on Pea's face, on the deep cut over his right eye, the swelling on his cheekbone, the blood in his eyeball – trying to find some clues.

'Hangin' out wit' you, I 'spect,' said Pea.

'So you told him we were mates now?' said Tokes, dabbing at the cut round Little Pea's eye. 'You told him you quit the gang?'

'Don't be stupid – I not suicidal, man.'

'You showed him the stuff on the camera?' I asked again.

'Enough with the interrogation.' Little Pea grinned then shivered a bit more. 'Can't you see I in a critical condition here? Probably got internal injuries too! I might be dyin'.'

Pea lifted up his top and I angled my camera in on his torso. There were three round red marks that looked a lot like cigarette burns. There were older marks there too, the same size and shape. And several purple red bruises, fist-shaped, still blossoming.

Tokes stared in horror. 'Why the hell do you keep hanging with those guys?'

'What's it to you anyway?' said Pea, tugging down his T-shirt and burying himself inside Tokes's hoodie. Only his eyes were visible, dancing with, what – fear, mischief, laughter? I couldn't tell.

'Why did you call us anyway?' said Tokes.

'I was only tryin' to help. Wit' your film, you know? I figured this would be good footage. Hey,' he said, turning to me. 'You like how I got my caller ID on your phone? Wanna know how I did it?'

'I don't believe you,' said Tokes, ignoring Pea's attempts to change the subject. 'Did Shiv send you here?'

'Nah, man!' said Pea quickly. Too quickly?

'Why'd you call her then?' Tokes nodded at me. 'Haven't you got any other mates?'

'Dunno,' said Pea sulkily. 'Just cos.' His face was edgy again, nervous. He looked round like a rodent that'd sensed a predator. 'Mebbe I jus' wanna show off my phone-hacking skills, innit. It take a super-phone-pirate to get into your contacts, you know?'

Tokes had stopped tending to Pea's wounds and was staring at him suspiciously.

'Anyways, I bring your camera back, dittn't I?' Pea squeaked. 'I dittn't have to do that. Coulda shown it to Shiv.'

'We still don't know for sure you didn't,' I said.

'Oh, you'd know if I had,' said Pea with a glint in his eye. 'That stuff with your mamma. Think what'd happen if I put that up on YouTube!' His eyes were darting brightly from one of us to the other as Tokes shot me a questioning look which I ignored.

'An' I coulda flogged the camera, made myself some cash,' Pea went on. 'But I bring it back to you, innit. Like a good friend.'

'Why'd you even take it then?' said Tokes.

'Cos knowledge is power, T-man,' said Pea solemnly. 'An' I was curious to know what you actually got on Shiv, innit.'

'So you can blackmail us with it?'

'Look, if you don't trust me, T-man, I got better places to be,' said Pea, throwing off Tokes's hoodie. His eyes were wild and he seemed kind of crazy, like a puppet on a string.

'You need to go to a doctor,' Tokes said.

'Don't trust doctors, me!' said Pea. 'No better than da police. No better than politicians.' He winked at me as he said that.

'You trust anyone, Pea?' asked Tokes.

'That be tellin'!' said Pea. His face looked childish, pouting, slightly scared. 'Lookee, I don't need this,' he declared, standing up on wobbly legs. 'I got other mates.'

'How many times do I have to tell you?' said Tokes. 'The Starfish Gang aren't your mates.'

Pea turned round angrily. 'What do you know? You don't got a clue 'bout my life, North London boy. I got mates, me. You'll see. An' you'll wish you was one of them too soon enough – jus' see if you don't.'

He lurched towards the gap in the fence, his steps drunken and unsteady, blood still trickling down his ear.

'Pea, wait!' said Tokes.

But he was already squeezing through. His voice wobbled slightly as he turned round and called, 'Jus' remember I bring you that camera back. I dittn't need to do that. Jus' remember.'

And then he was gone.

'Should we go after him?' I said.

Tokes was staring at the hole in the fence. He looked puzzled, like there was something he couldn't quite figure out. 'I dunno,' he said quietly, picking up his hoodie and shoving it back into his rucksack. 'Who knows what he's up to.' He sighed and the gutted expression flashed across his face, just like in the park the first time he saved Little Pea. 'But we've got no choice now. We've got to find out what his game is.'

'Why?'

'Cos I think it's probably my fault he got beaten up,' Tokes said, biting his lip. 'So it's down to me to sort it out.' He turned and looked at me. 'You coming? I mean, you don't have to . . .' He hesitated. 'I can go on my own.'

'I'm coming,' I said quickly.

He smiled then and I remember thinking, as he stood in a shaft of dusty sunlight, that he was probably the most beautiful boy I had ever seen. And that I'd go anywhere with him if he asked me.

We squeezed out from under the corrugated iron and stood blinking in the blinding light. The first thing I saw was Little Pea. He hadn't run off; he was still lingering under the arches, perched up on a giant council wheelie bin next to a load of posters advertising a 'Jesus miracle night' at the Church of Blessed Babylon. He looked like he'd been waiting for us. I called out, but when he saw us he jumped down off the bin and darted away, into the station.

'He's definitely up to something,' said Tokes.

I flicked my camera on. When you watch that bit back, you can see the shaking movement of our footsteps as we follow Little Pea past the fish factory, under the arches and into Coronation Road Station.

It's a funny little world down there, in the gloom under the platform. There's a doorway leading up some grubby steps to a dental surgery which claims to do the 'Cheapest root canals in the UK', next to a travel agent's crammed into a space the size of a broom cupboard. There are plantain skins and food wrappers lying all over the floor and the whole place is plastered with fly-posters, some offering to save your soul, some trying to sell miracle skin creams, others for gigs and raves and comedy nights. Some of the posters are new and lurid, still flapping in the wind, others so faded they look as if they've been there since the Queen and her sister came visiting during the Blitz.

I caught sight of Pea again, dancing round by the Italian restaurant on the other side of the station entrance, but he disappeared as soon as he saw I'd clocked him.

Tokes didn't seem to have noticed he was there. 'Oh no! That's all we need!' he was muttering.

He'd slowed to a halt and was staring over to where two police officers were standing outside the entrance to the station. One was on his radio, while the other was looking around, like he was watching out for someone.

'What's the matter?'

'They just make me nervous, that's all,' he said.

'But we haven't done anything.'

'That doesn't necessarily make a difference.'

I glanced round. I couldn't see Little Pea any more – he'd ghosted himself away – and one of the policemen was saying something into his headpiece about things kicking off down at the station. The other one, who looked like he'd had a broken nose, was now staring over at us.

'Come on then,' Tokes said, his jaw tightening. 'Looks weird if we just stand here.'

And then he slipped his hand into mine. He didn't look down or say anything. He just did it, like it was the most natural thing in the world.

The policeman with the broken nose gave a sort of grin, but Tokes kept walking, staring right ahead, his face set in grim determination.

My heart was starting to beat really fast as I remembered the story he'd told me. About the time he'd gone out for milk and been handcuffed. And the feeling of his fingers, warm and sticky against mine, made my head spin oddly.

We were nearly past when the first officer said, 'Uh, can you wait up a minute there, son?'

'For real?' Tokes tightened his grip on my hand, but his face betrayed no fear at all as he turned round slowly.

'Yeah, son. For real!' said Broken Nose, glancing at Tokes and then at me, like he was trying to figure us out, work out what we were doing together. 'Can you empty your pockets, please?'

I waited for him to ask me too, but he didn't.

'He's with me,' I murmured.

Broken Nose just looked me up and down. 'If you say so, miss.'

I remember how he said that word 'miss'. How it annoyed me that he was doing this to Tokes, but he was being all polite to me at the same time. Sometimes parallel universes can be about the colour of skin too, I remember thinking.

'This isn't fair!' I stammered.

'Life ain't fair,' said the first policeman. 'Empty your pockets, son.'

Tokes looked at the floor, hand still tightly clasping mine, and said, 'On what grounds?'

'Why aren't you asking me to empty my pockets?' I said.

'Look, miss. Jus' keep out of this, OK?'

'On what grounds?' Tokes asked again. His voice was calm, but I could see from his eyes that he was worried – or mad. Maybe both. 'I know the law. You have to give grounds, show me your ID, read me the act about stop-and-search and that.'

'You a lawyer now, son?'

'I just know my rights, that's all.'

'Well, then you know about special licences. We got a licence to stop-and-search this whole area today,' said Broken Nose. 'Spot checks. No grounds needed.'

The camera was still rolling in the pouch around my neck, but the policemen were too busy harassing Tokes to notice. On the footage mostly all you can see is boots and bits of people's legs, the odd flash of a face. The audio is still a bit fuzzy, but you can make out the sound of the station announcer running like a soundtrack in the background, and people walking past, talking about their day, like nothing is happening.

'Why?' I asked. 'Why is there a special licence?'

'You watch the news, miss?'

The camera shakes at that point so you can tell I'm nodding.

'Then you'll know there's been a spot of bother round here the last few days,' Broken Nose said. His voice was patronising, but not as aggressive as when he talked to Tokes. 'We wanna keep a lid on it. Make sure it don't escalate.' He broke off for a second. 'I don't see you emptying those pockets, son,' he went on. 'I'm going to have to cuff you.'

'You can't cuff him!' My voice sounds weak and reedy on the film.

'Just leave it,' said Tokes, avoiding my gaze as he disentangled his fingers from mine and put his hands out for the officers to cuff.

'But it isn't right!' I protested, my fingers feeling empty without his.

He shrugged and I caught his face for a second. You can see his eyes. They look frightened and resigned.

Broken Nose was fiddling with the cuffs. On the film of this bit, Tokes looks really young, just a teenage kid being shoved around by two bully-boy police officers.

The first officer spun Tokes round and started turning out his pockets. People kept going in and out of the station, but none of them said anything. Most of them pretended not to notice.

'Can we see what's in your bag, son?' said Broken Nose and the way he said it, it wasn't really a question.

Tokes's face looked strained and there was a tinge of new colour in his cheeks as he shrugged off his rucksack and handed it to the policeman, who stuck his hand inside and pulled out the first-aid kit, an empty chip packet and a copy of *Great Expectations*.

'It's a good book,' said Tokes with half a smile on his face. 'You should read it.'

The officer glared at Tokes and I wanted to laugh out loud, but now he was tugging out Tokes's hoodie which was covered in little dots of Pea's blood.

Tokes's expression changed. 'I can explain that,' he said quickly.

'Oh yeah?' The policeman started rummaging around in the pockets. He reached into the inside pocket and his hand closed over something. 'And can you explain this?'

He drew out his hand and in it was a flick knife.

I caught that bit clearly on film. It's a bit fuzzy, but you can see the knife and Tokes staring at it. And this time he didn't laugh. Instead, his face changed completely. All the colour drained out of it and his eyes went bright, even in the gloom.

'That's not mine!'

'What do you need a knife for, son?'

'I don't!' Tokes insisted, his voice high and tight.

'What's it doing in your pocket then?'

'I don't know. Somebody must have put it there. I . . .' Then he smacked his lips together, shook his head and muttered, 'Pea!'

Suddenly I got it too. Little Pea wrapped up in Tokes's hoodie, saying he was cold. Pea leading us right into a trap . . .

Tokes's eyes were full of anger. He suddenly didn't seem bothered about the policeman who was demanding his name and address.

And all I could think was that he'd promised his mum he'd stay out of trouble, and now he was as deep into it as he could be.

'I'm afraid we're going to have to take you down to the station, son.'

'No,' I said. 'It isn't his.'

'Carrying a weapon is a criminal offence.'

'But it was planted.'

'Miss, you need to step aside and let us do our job.'

Tokes's face was a blank. Not angry or gutted, just blank. 'You should go, Maggie,' he said.

'No, I'm not leaving.'

'You promised you'd go if I told you to,' he said. 'And there's nothing you can do to help.'

I looked at him desperately. And I could see suddenly what he meant about me being safe in my world, even though it existed side by side with his. And it made me mad and sad and determined to do something about it.

'Call my mum,' I said suddenly.

'You what, kid?' said Broken Nose.

'My mum. She's Harriet Hatton. MP. You've heard of her, right? Call her. Here.' I handed him my mobile phone. 'Call her.'

SCENE 16: THE LOUNGE IN MAGGIE'S HOUSE

I was wrong about my mum.

I thought she'd come through for me. Because, whatever else, she's my mum and she's supposed to love me and look out for me. She might not be around much, but I figured she'd be there for me if I really needed her.

How wrong can you be?

The police called and told her they had taken me and Tokes down to the police station. She apologised for my behaviour then sent Petra to get me. Me not Tokes.

'I don't want you seeing that boy again,' was her opener as she walked through the door three hours later, mobile phone still pressed to her ear.

'But he didn't do anything,' I said, my voice dry as burned paper from shouting and crying while nobody listened.

She raised an eyebrow, half her attention still on the voice on the other end of the phone.

Then she lifted a single finger to silence me, and said in her sweetest voice to the person on the phone, 'Sorry about that! Yes? That sounds perfect!'

As she spoke in her silky voice to the caller, all I could think of was how the police had put cuffs on Tokes, but not touched me. How they'd bundled us both into the back of the police van and made us sit for hours in an interview room, making Tokes feel like a criminal and me like a nuisance. How Petra had dragged me out of there and made me leave Tokes – and how he might still be banged up in a cell for all I knew.

Finally, my mum hung up and turned to me. Her face looked clouded, like she'd briefly forgotten I was there.

'Who is this boy anyway?' she said, kicking off her shoes and facing me barefoot, eyes tired.

'He's my friend.'

'I thought you didn't have any friends,' she said, before quickly adding, 'I'm sorry. That came out wrong.' She sighed and ran her hand through her hair. 'I only meant I didn't think you really knew anyone around here.'

I glared down at my feet and didn't answer.

'Maggie,' she said softly, taking a step towards me across the thickly carpeted floor. I kept my eyes down because I could feel her willing me to look at her. 'Look, I'm struggling to understand how this all happened. How you came to be involved. What were you even doing with a boy like that?'

I glanced up. She was only a few metres away, near enough for me to see that her lipstick had worn off round the edges.

'You don't even know Tokes,' I said. 'He's really clever. Top of the class at his school. He knows more long words than anyone I've ever met. Reads books all the time. He wants to be a lawyer or a doctor, to help people.'

'And yet he was found with a knife in his possession,' she said. Her eyebrows were raised as she said it.

'It wasn't his.'

She sighed again as her phone beeped in her hand.

'Hadn't you better get that?' I said.

'Maggie, if you did this to get my attention then you've got it,' she said quietly, firmly, ignoring the phone. 'One hundred per cent.'

'I didn't *do* anything,' I said. 'Neither did Tokes. We were set up.'

'OK,' she said, 'I'm listening. Tell me. Tell me what happened.' She sat down on the pouffe in the middle of the room. She looked funny perched there in her stockinged feet.

And I thought then about telling her everything: about the fight in the park, about Pea telling Shiv that the police hurt Pats, about Tokes turning down a place in the Starfish Gang. I had a feeling that once I started talking I might not be able to stop. That other stuff would come out, stuff I'd been holding in for so long it seemed to fill up my head, my whole body sometimes.

'I'm trying to understand, Maggie,' Mum insisted. 'But I can't if you won't talk to me.'

And then I remembered Tokes's face when I'd left him in the police station. The sunshine gone from his eyes, his shoulders sagging, jaw tight with anxiety. 'Don't worry, Maggie,' he'd said. 'I'll be fine.' I'd trusted her to help and she'd made me leave him there all on his own. And I didn't think I could ever forgive her for that.

So I bit my lip and said nothing. And the room seemed to hum with unspoken words as she stared at me and I stared at the floor and refused to talk.

Eventually, she said, 'Look, I know you think I work too hard. That I'm never there for you when you need me. But I'm here now.' She paused. 'I'm supposed to be meeting with the head of the Police Complaints Commission, but I came home instead. For you.'

I don't know what she expected me to say to that, but my face felt tight with tears and my throat was too scratched and raw to speak even if I'd wanted to.

She exhaled slowly. 'Is this about your father leaving?'

I shook my head, but she didn't seem to notice.

'Because I know you blame me for what happened,' she went on. 'But your father left me too, Maggie.'

'This isn't about Dad,' I muttered.

She still wasn't listening. 'Marriages are complicated, but I'm not going to bad-mouth your dad just to make you like me more.'

'Why not?' I said in a choked voice. 'That's what you politicians do to your opponents, isn't it?'

I looked up and saw her shake her head, her brow furrowed, as if confused by what I was saying. 'This isn't politics; this is your dad, Maggie,' she said softly. 'And I'm not going to drag you into taking sides. If that means you blame me and feel the need to punish me by doing stuff like this . . .'

'How many times,' I whispered, lowering my eyes again. 'I didn't *do* anything.'

'Maggie, I know how hard the divorce has been on you.' She leaned forward then and put her hand on mine, curled her perfectly manicured fingers over my bloodstained, stubby ones. I let my hand rest there for a moment, feeling the warmth of her skin melting into mine. She shifted so she was kneeling on the floor in front of me and, again, I could almost feel her willing me to look up. I think I almost did.

'All this acting out,' she went on. 'I know it's your way of dealing with what happened.'

I pulled my hand away quickly, wrapping my arms round my body and tucking my fingers under my armpits. I didn't trust myself to look at her at all because I knew I'd cry, and I was determined not to let her see me crumble.

'And I want to help, Maggie. But I need you to talk to me.'

'I don't want to talk to you,' I said, my voice gravelly with locked-in tears. 'I just want to know what's going to happen to Tokes.'

She tipped back on her knees then and gave a long, slow sigh, staring up at the elaborate crystal light fitting which my dad had always hated.

'They put cuffs on him, Mum!' I said quietly.

'And they are within their rights to do so,' she said, shaking her head and fixing me with one of her 'I'm-too-tired-to-deal-with-this-right-now' looks.

I could feel my eyes starting to throb again, so I screwed up my mouth and said, 'Since when are the police allowed to stop-and-search a teenager just because they feel like it?'

'It's the law,' she said simply, chewing her lip and rocking back on to her stockinged feet so that there was distance between us again.

'Then it's a stupid law!'

She breathed deeply, staring at my hair critically like she'd only just noticed it. I'd plaited it into cornrows down one side of my head and hung feathers down the other side, but she didn't comment on it.

'Well, we have a situation in the neighbourhood that could blow up at any moment.'

I thought of what we'd seen down at the police station. The

crowd of people with banners saying stuff like *Justice for Pats Karunga* and *We Want the Truth*, their faces angry, war in their eyes. I remembered Tokes saying, 'It only takes a little spark to start a fire.'

'You need to say there'll be an inquiry,' I said, my voice still choked. 'That's what Tokes says. He says people think you're covering up for the police and that will only make it worse.'

She raised her eyebrows. 'Well, your friend Tokes could have a point there,' she said, with a wry smile.

'And it won't calm things down if the police go around harassing innocent people either,' I said.

She nodded, stroking her forehead again. 'That is also a valuable point, Maggie. But when it comes to your friend Tokes the police had been given a tip-off that he was carrying a weapon. They had a duty to act on that.'

'A tip-off?' My head jerked up. 'From who?'

'You know I couldn't tell you even if I knew myself,' she said. She stood up then, wobbling slightly as she got to her feet. And it felt like a moment had passed – been missed somehow – and it was too late to get it back.

'Mum!' I said quickly. 'What's going to happen to Tokes?'

She looked down at me and hesitated for just a second. Her eyes were on my hair. 'Maggie, I really do not want you seeing that boy again.'

'But what will happen to him?'

Another pause, a glance over at the shelves full of books that nobody ever reads – except Tokes. 'He'll probably get a caution.'

'What does that mean?'

'It means if he offends again he'll be charged and sentenced,' she said simply.

'But he wanted a new start. He promised his mum,' I started to say.

'Then I imagine he and his mother will be having a very similar conversation to this one, don't you?' she said. She closed her eyes for a moment and put her fingers to her temples. 'I wonder if theirs will be any more successful.'

I didn't reply.

Her phone beeped and she flicked it open to view a new message, her attention away from me again.

'I asked you for your help,' I said quietly.

She looked up quickly, phone already halfway to her ear. 'Yes, you did. And I love you, Maggie, and you may not think I'm helping by saying this, but it's my job to protect you. So you will not see that boy again, and that is me helping you, do you understand?'

She stood there, across the lounge from me, and I really felt like I hated her then – more than I ever had before or ever would again.

I was wrong about that too.

SCENE 17: TOKES'S BEDSIT

Maybe that's why I let everything else happen. Because I was so mad at her.

The first thing I did next morning was go round to see Tokes, because he didn't have a phone and I had no way of knowing if he was even OK. And because I'd spent all night awake or tossing in and out of dreams, remembering his face when I left him at the police station, wondering if he'd ever speak to me again.

Tokes had told me where he lived, but I'd never been there. I think maybe he'd been too embarrassed to take me. It was only a few streets away from our house, round by the back of the bus station, just off Coronation Road. A tall, battered-looking building, with a key-cutting shop underneath it and a modern block of flats next to it.

As I went past Choudhary's Electrical Store, Mr Choudhary waved to me and beckoned me in.

'So? Did it work?' he asked excitedly as I stepped inside. The sun glancing off all the glass display cases made it seem like an exotic treasure trove that day.

'It was good.' I nodded. 'Worked perfectly.'

I glanced around. Ishmael was nowhere to be seen. Mr Choudhary was busy fiddling with the CCTV monitor but he stopped now, his eyes twinkling.

'Aha! I knew it!' he said. 'So many clever advances in technology – something new every day. Soon I will be left far behind while you and Ishmael zoom around on flying cars with microchips embedded in your brains.'

I giggled. It felt like the first time I'd laughed in days. Mr Choudhary pulled out something wrapped in a piece of greaseproof paper from beneath the counter. He glanced around as if on the lookout for spies as he unwrapped it and offered me a piece of cake.

'Mrs Choudhary's famous honey cake,' he whispered. 'She does not know I snuck it out of the house this morning. I am supposed to be watching my weight.' He patted his round stomach. 'Perhaps you will help me out by sharing it with me.'

'Thank you,' I said, breaking off a piece and letting the sweet taste trickle into my mouth.

Mr Choudhary tipped his head to one side like a bird. 'So I expect your mother has told you to keep away from the police station today?' he said, popping a bit of cake into his mouth with a smile. He gestured at the TV screens which were showing footage of the crowd – twice as big as it had been yesterday.

I nodded, but didn't tell him I'd been at the police station myself the day before.

'There's going to be trouble, I fear. Ishmael is buying new padlocks for the grille, just in case. And I am making sure the CCTV camera is working shipshape.' He smiled and I saw that there were crumbs of cake in his moustache. 'Sometimes I think that boy is in charge here and not I!' he said, but his eyes sparkled as if the thought pleased him.

'Do you think the trouble will spread up here?' I asked.

Mr Choudhary frowned. 'Who knows, but better safe than sorry is my motto. This shop is our family livelihood. We are not taking any chances. Now you keep yourself safe, Miss Maggie, do you hear me?'

'You too,' I said. And I left with the taste of honey on my lips and the image of him checking the security camera in my mind.

In the thick heat of the morning, food smells seemed to choke the air on Coronation Road: stale kebabs, fresh fish turning in the sunshine, fried chicken, candyfloss, biltong. When I got to Tokes's building, I suddenly wasn't sure what to do. So I took my camera out and filmed it from outside: the ornate cornicing above the key shop, now grimy and crumbling, the way the building ended abruptly. 'Probably bomb damage,' I imagined my dad saying. He hadn't called – even though Mum had emailed him about what happened.

Finally, I took a deep breath, tucked my camera in my pocket and rang the buzzer. Nobody answered for a bit and I nearly turned away. Then a crackle of static and a woman's voice came over the intercom.

'Who is this?'

'It's Maggie,' I said. 'Tokes's friend.'

There was a pause then the sound of muffled voices on the other end. Then Tokes.

'What do you want, Maggie?'

The sound of his voice made something knock in my chest – relief and something else.

'I came to check you were OK.'

A pause. 'I'm fine.'

I stood there, my fingers twisting through the short tufts of purple on my head. 'And I want to say sorry for leaving you there.' I paused. 'Can I come up?'

'You sure that's a good idea?' His voice was tinny and cracked over the intercom.

I thought of my mum telling me that she didn't want me to see him again.

'Yes,' I lied.

Another pause, a crackle of static on the intercom. 'OK. We're in number four.'

The buzzer sounded and I pushed open the door to a dank-smelling communal hallway. The bedsit was on the third floor so I made my way up several flights of dusty stairs then knocked on the door marked 4. Tokes opened it and stood in the doorway, blocking it like he didn't really want me to see inside.

'Hi,' I said.

'Hi.' He seemed older this morning, no sunshine in his eyes.

'Can I come in?' I asked.

'If you really want to.' I couldn't quite make out the expression on his face. His jaw was tense as he opened the door and ushered me in.

I didn't want to be shocked when I stepped in, but I couldn't help it. He'd said I had no idea what it's like to be poor and for the first time I properly believed him. I'd thought he was joking when he said his home was half the size of our kitchen, but it turned out to be true. The entire bedsit was about the size of my bedroom. There was a large double bed in the middle of the room and one of those foldaway beds wedged up against the bay window. Two open suitcases stood by the wall and there was more stuff all over the bed. In the corner, next to a tiny sink, was a rusty two-ring camping stove and a fridge the size of a hotel minibar that hummed noisily. I glanced around for a doorway or a second room, but there was none. This was it.

'Home sweet home,' Tokes muttered. I glanced at him. His chin was up and his eyes were bright.

I wanted to say something, but I had no idea what.

Then I noticed Tokes's mum on the other side of the room, caught in a shaft of dusty sunshine coming through the dirty lace curtains. She wasn't anything like I expected. She was really tiny and young. She didn't look much older than a teenager herself, except she had these tired eyes that could have belonged to a granny.

'Mum,' said Tokes. 'This is Maggie, who I told you about.'

'Hello,' I said and suddenly I wished I hadn't come empty-handed. I wished I'd brought the doughnuts or flowers or something.

But Tokes's mum smiled and said, 'It's nice to meet you, Maggie. I'm grateful for what you did for my boy.'

She came over and put a hand on Tokes's arm and he smiled at her almost shyly. I liked the way he looked at her. Like she was precious somehow, breakable. But like he was proud of her too.

'Oh . . . I didn't,' I stammered. 'I was trying to help. I thought my mum could sort things, but . . .' I tailed off.

'You tried,' she said quietly. 'That was nice.'

I glanced around. The wallpaper looked like it had been put up last century with its faded floral pattern, peeling in places and covered in damp patches. The carpet seemed almost as old. The stark geometric pattern was now covered in dark spots and dust.

'My Tokes say to me that you are making a film,' Tokes's mum said, glancing from her son to me. She wasn't sure about me, but she was giving me a chance, I thought. For some reason that made me feel really sad.

'Um, yes,' I said.

'He also say you are a very talented film-maker.'

'Tokes is doing the hard bit,' I said. 'He's writing the script. I'm just doing the pictures. He's really –' I stopped. 'He's a really good writer.'

She smiled at Tokes, pride in her eyes. 'Yes, he is a good boy. A good son,' she said simply. I watched the way she put a hand on Tokes's face. Just a little touch and a smile. It made me even sadder.

'Will you excuse me, Maggie,' she said in her soft, lilting voice. 'I must wash before I go to work or I still smell of chip fat.'

She crossed the room and I stepped out of the way to let her on to the landing where I guessed the bathroom must be. Did they have to share it with the people who lived in the other bedsits?

Tokes went to draw back the curtains to let more grubby light spill into the room. 'She's got a cleaning job up at the hospital,' he explained quietly. 'She works three jobs now: the burger bar, the hospital and she does the late-night cleaning shift in an office block too. The rest of the time she sleeps. Just to pay for this place.'

I nodded, but said nothing.

'I guess you want to film it, right?' he said, eyes still not meeting mine.

'What?'

'Here. The bedsit.'

'Oh, only if you want me to.'

'Well, we don't want the whole world thinking I live in the lap of luxury, now do we!' He grinned, but it didn't quite reach his eyes. 'They might get jealous.'

'Sure,' I said, tugging the camera out of my pocket and flicking it on. I ran it once round the room before turning it on to Tokes.

'We had a proper flat before. Proper stuff. My mum had to leave everything behind.' Then he added, 'It's because of me that we had to come here. It's my fault.'

He looked up at me, like he wanted to check I understood, and I nodded because I didn't know what else to say or do.

'My mum got pregnant with me while she and dad were at college.' He glanced down at the swirling patterns on the carpet as he spoke. 'She was training to be a pharmacist and Dad wanted to be a mechanic, but he dropped out and tried to get a job to support her. He had no qualifications though.' He paused for a second. 'That's how he ended up joining the crew – doing what he does. Because of me.'

I focused the camera on the curve of his neck and his scrunched-up shoulders as he continued to stare at the floor.

'The thing is, my mum was always telling me to work hard,' he went on. 'Not to let anything get in the way of my education. She said education was my ticket to a better life.' He glanced over at the doorway through which his mum had just left, his face tight with concentration as he spoke. 'But when you live on an estate, and you got a dad in the business, you can't be invisible forever.'

'You don't have to tell me all this, you know,' I said quietly.

'I know,' he said, and he looked up and held my eye for a moment. 'But I want to. So you understand.'

And I didn't understand – not really. Not then and maybe not now. But I think he needed to tell me, to have a record of his mum's sacrifice, so the world would know what she'd done for him. So I just kept the camera rolling and let him talk.

'My dad's crew use lots of the kids on the estate to do drops for them,' he said, his lips tightening as he spoke. 'Little kids on bikes making deliveries don't attract the attention of the police, you know?'

He looked at me again and I nodded quickly.

'My mum told my dad she didn't want me involved. Never. He was to keep me out of it. She made me promise too.'

I kept watching him through the viewfinder as he spoke. The dusty light fell over his face, making him look different, ghostly somehow, and older. 'Are you sure you want me to film this?'

He looked up, nodded quickly, then kept talking. 'But one day a crew member turned up outside my school. Him and my dad never got on so well. I think it was a power thing. He was showing my dad he could get to him through me.'

He met my eye for a second and I blinked, but didn't look away.

'When he asked me to take a parcel for him, I said no.' Tokes looked down again, his brow creased. 'But he wouldn't leave it. After that, every day when I came out of school he'd be there. He said I needed to take a side. That I was either with the crew or against them. Then he started talking about my mum . . .'

He looked quickly in the direction his mum had gone and his eyes were clouded with something between love and fear.

'What did you do?'

'I told my dad,' said Tokes, his face crumpling as he spoke. 'I thought he could make it stop.'

'Did he?' I asked, zooming in to his face so you could see the anxiety in his dark eyes.

He shook his head. 'I knew things weren't right when he came home with his face bashed so bad he needed twelve stitches. He said it was a rival gang, but I knew he was lying. So I –' He hesitated. His eyes were half-closed and staring down at the duvet cover. Suddenly I felt as if I shouldn't be filming.

He paused for a long time before saying, 'So I started doing deliveries.'

He said the words so simply, then he looked right at the camera, twisting his lip a little.

'Drugs?'

He nodded his head, but didn't look at me. 'I guess. I never asked.'

I tried not to look shocked, and I kept filming even though it didn't feel right any more. 'How long did you do it for?' I asked.

'Not long. My mum found out. She moved us here the very same night.' He paused, looked away from the camera. 'And that's it. That's why we're here. That's why I've got to look after my mum now because she hasn't got anyone else. And she gave up everything to save me.'

Neither of us said anything for a moment. I panned my camera round the room again, lingering for ages on the sun shining patterns on to the lurid carpet.

'And that's why you want to help Little Pea?' I said.

Tokes shrugged. 'My mum and I look out for each other,' he said. 'Not every kid is lucky enough to have someone like that.'

I nodded, thinking of my mum's fingers on mine, staring at me. Would she give up everything for me like Tokes's mum had done?

I must have been quiet for longer than I thought because finally he said, 'I'll understand if you want to go.'

I looked up quickly. 'Why would I go?'

'After what I told you.' He had that bright-eyed look again. 'Now you know I was running drugs. I would understand if you wanted out.'

My face was flushed and I let the camera drop to my side, but it was still recording. When you look back on that bit, you can just hear our voices against the swirling pattern on the carpet. 'Do you *want* me to leave?' I asked.

'I don't expect your mum wants you hanging out with someone like me.'

'She doesn't,' I said with a small smile.

'And it's like I told you. I'm a magnet for trouble.' He kicked a foot against the carpet. 'Look at what happened yesterday. You got dragged in because of me.'

'It wasn't your fault,' I said. 'It was Pea who set you up.'

He stared at the floor intently as he asked, 'When the police guy first found that knife, did you think it was mine?'

'No!' I said quickly.

His eyes flicked up to my face. 'Cos I wouldn't blame you if you did.'

'I knew it wasn't yours,' I said again.

He kept looking at me. 'Thanks. And, you know, thanks for sticking up for me.'

'Fat lot of use it was!' I muttered, feeling my skin heat up.

'That's not the point.' His brown pebble eyes held my gaze. 'Don't you understand? Apart from my mum, nobody ever did anything like that for me before.'

I was aware that there were only a few centimetres of dusty air between us. The sound of my heart beating was loud in my ears.

'You'd have done the same for me,' I said softly. 'For Little Pea even.'

'But you *could* have walked away and you didn't.'

There was a moment's awkward silence. We stood there looking at each other and something seemed to hover between us. Then he grinned and the moment passed. 'In fact, I think I remember *telling* you to walk away.'

I remembered the camera in my hand and focused it on my cherry-red boots. 'Like I was going to do what you said!'

'No one tells Maggie what to do, right? I saw how much fuss you kicked up at the police station.'

I smiled awkwardly, keeping my eyes averted from his. 'My voice hurts like mad from all the shouting,' I said. 'Did you get cautioned?'

He nodded.

'So what are we going to do then?' I said, tracing the patterns on the wallpaper now with the camera lens.

'Nothing,' said Tokes. 'Turn the other cheek, my mum said.'

'But –'

He looked up. 'She's right,' he said. 'Pea only did it cos Shiv made him. And maybe now Shiv's shown us who's boss he'll leave us alone.'

'Maybe, but . . .'

'If we retaliate, it won't stop.'

The word 'retaliate' seemed to sparkle in the dusty rays of sunshine. Another one of Tokes's words, long and out of place, but part of who he was.

'But if you don't do anything they've won, haven't they?'

He looked at me again, his eyes seeming to search my face for a moment. 'I'm not bothered about winning, cos I'm not playing their game, Maggie.'

I hesitated for a second, taking this in. Then I smiled and said, 'Well, you might not want to show Pea, but I can.'

'You?'

'He won't be expecting it from me, will he?'

He looked anxious for a moment then he laughed like what I'd said was really funny. 'Expecting what? You gonna tool him?'

I shrugged. It all sounded silly – me acting like I was the heroine in some movie – when anyone could see I wasn't even remotely the leading lady type. I mean, since when did heroines have multicoloured hair and Buzz Lightyear T-shirts?

'I'm telling you, Maggie. You want to walk away from all this,' Tokes said, more serious now. 'It's not your fight.'

'It is now! I owe you one for leaving you at the police station.'

The air between us seemed to vibrate again and my stomach lurched like it always did when Ishmael Choudhary caught me looking at him. Only this was different somehow, because Tokes was looking right back at me and his eyes were dark with something I couldn't quite understand.

Then his face broke into a grin and I couldn't help smiling back. He had the kind of smile that lit you up inside no matter what else was going on.

'Guess we're stuck with each other for a bit in that case!' he said.

'Guess so.'

Just then there was a beep from the bed next to where Tokes was standing. He picked up a battered-looking mobile – his mum's I guessed – and glanced at it. His face went pale.

'What is it?' I asked.

He bit his lip and looked for a second as if he was going to be sick. 'It's my dad,' he said.

Tokes's mum came back in at that moment. She was wearing one of those cleaners' tabards and her hair was tied up in a ponytail which made her look even younger.

'Are you going to work on the film with your friend today?' she asked, smiling at me, then at Tokes, and running a hand over his head again. It looked kind of funny because he was a lot taller than her.

Then she reached for her phone.

'Mum . . .' he said, then he hesitated. He looked at her the way I saw my mum looking at me sometimes, his face filled with concern.

'Dad sent you a text,' he finished.

Tokes's mum flicked open her phone and read the message.

'How'd he get your new number?' asked Tokes.

'I gave it to him,' she said quietly.

'Does he know where we are?'

She shook her head, then pocketed her phone quickly. 'Never mind,' she said. 'Don't you worry about him. You go and have fun.'

But Tokes did look worried, and I think that's when I got it. He felt he needed to look after her, protect her – that he was the man of the house now.

'But, Mum . . .'

'Don't worry,' she said, her eyes meeting his like she understood. 'Everything will be fine, boy. Just remember what I say to you last night, eh?'

'Sure, yeah, but . . .'

She had to stand on tiptoes to plant a quick kiss on her tall son's cheek. She stroked his face as she did so and I watched her fingers run over his skin as if memorising it.

'An' keep away from the police station,' she added in a soft, lilting voice. 'I hear on the radio there's going to be trouble there today. You keep away, you hear?'

'Sure,' said Tokes with a nod.

She stopped and looked at me and said, 'It was very nice to meet you, Maggie.' Then she turned to Tokes and said, 'Make me proud, boy.'

'Mum,' Tokes called after her as she walked towards the door.

'Yes?'

I could see Tokes looking at her handbag, where the phone was. 'Is Dad OK?'

She hesitated and I watched her face; it looked like she was in pain and pretending not to be. Suddenly it felt wrong for me to be there.

'He's fine,' she said quietly, after a long moment.

'How would we know if he wasn't?' asked Tokes. 'How

would we know if anything happened to him?'

She looked Tokes right in the eyes and said, 'Don' worry 'bout your daddy. He made his choices. Now it your turn to make yours.'

SCENE 18: CORONATION ROAD

Tokes suggested going to the library. 'We can work on the film there,' he said as we emerged into the blinding sunshine, which was a shock to the senses after the dinginess of the bedsit.

There was a weird vibe on Coronation Road as we made our way to the library. It was quieter than usual, except for an old drunk sitting outside the chemist's, yelling, 'Reclaim the streets! Kill the pigs!' And a couple of girls in tight velour tracksuits were laughing at him and throwing chips in his direction. Some of the shops still had their shutters half down and, as we walked past the window of Choudhary's Electrical Store, the six huge TV screens were showing new footage from outside the police station where the crowd had swelled to maybe a couple of hundred people. There were even more banners: *We Want the Truth!* and *Arrest Police Thugs* and *Stop the Cover-up*. In the back of the shot you could see that some of the shopkeepers in the parade opposite the police station had closed up completely, and pulled down their barricades as if they anticipated trouble.

'You can hear them,' said Tokes. 'Listen.'

He was right. Behind the rumble of London traffic we could hear the shouts of the crowd. The police station was a few streets away, but it sounded closer.

I glanced past the window into the shop. Ishmael was there and so was Mr Choudhary. Ishmael waved and I waved back, my face suddenly aflame.

Tokes glanced at me. 'Is that your friend who helped with the camera?'

'Yup,' I said quickly, but the heat in my cheeks wouldn't go away and I could feel Tokes frowning next to me and I wanted to explain, but I couldn't.

'Let's go to the police station!' I said, changing the subject instead. 'We could film what happens.'

'Maggie, no way . . .'

'For the movie,' I said. 'I mean, maybe this is the ending.'

'Maggie, my mum . . .'

'I know, but –'

'Please, Maggie. Can we just try to stay out of trouble for one day at least?'

I glanced at the pictures of the crowd on the giant TV screens. There was something in the way they looked, like they were about to bubble over or go up in flames. I wanted to keep watching. I wanted to be there to film when the whole thing went up. But I glanced at Tokes and saw the anxiety etched all over his face, and suddenly I just wanted to help keep him safe, so I turned away and followed him towards the library.

The minute we stepped inside it felt calm. The multicoloured glass made the streets outside seem a million miles away. It even made my mum seem more distant. For once the smell of books was reassuring too.

We made our way over to the computer area and spent ages fiddling with our film footage. Tokes had written this voice-over script which he read to me in a whisper. It was good. I could see the pictures he was drawing with it, and how they tied in with stuff we'd filmed. He'd included bits of songs too, and some stuff from books he'd read. He'd even used a bit from the book he'd borrowed from my house.

'Cos it's about this poor kid who meets this rich girl who lives with this old cobwebby lady. The girl kind of weaves a web around him – of lies and stuff – and he gets caught up in it and falls in love with her.' He said the last bit really quickly and I felt myself blushing.

'Oh. Right. What happens?'

'He does whatever it takes to become rich, to try and be like her, but it ruins his life,' he said simply, staring hard at the screen. 'Because it sort of turns out he can't change where he came from anyway.'

We were sitting side by side, our knees almost touching.

'Do you believe that then?' I said. 'That you can't really change. That where you come from makes you who you are?'

'I dunno,' he said, staring at the image of Little Pea dancing in the gallery, frozen on the screen. 'Sometimes I do, but my mum says you can't think like that. That anyone can change if they really want to.'

'Even Shiv?' I said.

Tokes stared at the picture of Pea, his face grinning, his eyes bright, and I remembered the way Shiv had held the knife up against his shiny skin in the park.

'I dunno. Maybe you can leave it too late. Get trapped.'

I glanced up quickly at his face, and I wondered if he was actually thinking about his dad when he said that.

'So what happens at the end of the book?' I said. 'Does the boy manage to change? And what happens to the rich girl? Do they . . .' I hesitated. 'Do they get together?'

'Oh, I haven't finished it yet,' he said quickly, looking down at his hands on the keyboard. 'I'll tell you when I do.'

And that was how our film felt too: unfinished. Like it needed the car chase, the fight scene, the bit where the whole story explodes in front of your eyes. It felt like our big finale was just out of reach, hanging in the hot air, and it made me restless, jumpy.

'What do you think will happen?' I said.

Tokes shrugged. 'I dunno exactly.'

I looked at the screen again. Little Pea grinned out at me – like he knew exactly what was going to happen, but wasn't going to tell us.

Tokes sighed again as if he could read my mind. 'Look, I bet we can see the police station from up here. Why don't we go and check it out. Then if anything happens we can film from above.'

'I suppose,' I said.

'I can't risk getting in trouble, Maggie. You get that, right? I'm on a caution.'

I nodded.

'Come on then, Hollywood,' he said, grinning and flinging a casual arm round my shoulders as he used Pea's name for me. 'Let's go get some aerial footage!'

So we made our way over to the big glass windows and that's when I caught sight of Little Pea. He was sitting on a windowsill in the Military History section, peering out into the hot afternoon. He was curled up into a ball and it looked almost as if he was asleep, but he obviously wasn't because he jumped up the moment he saw us.

'Hello, peeps!' he squeaked, glancing nervously in the direction of the windows like he thought we were going to send him flying out of one.

'What are you doing here?' asked Tokes, eyeing him furiously.

'It's a library, innit.' Pea giggled nervously. 'I'm reading my way through da classics, me.'

Tokes narrowed his eyes and looked around. From the window next to us there was a view right over the Starfish Estate and the police station where the crowd had grown even more, spreading out over the High Street now, holding up the traffic. 'Are you following us again?'

'No way. What you think I am, a stalker?'

'You set Tokes up,' I said. 'And got him cautioned.' My voice came out louder than I meant it to and from over at the desk one of the librarians glared at me.

'That wasn't me,' Pea whispered, his eyes wide, but his face looking anything but innocent. 'The knife, it . . .'

'How do you even know it was a knife if it wasn't you?' Tokes said.

Pea gave one of his little wiggles, blinked about six times and said, 'OK, look, it was me. But I gotta do it, right. Shiv nearly half killed me – you seed that.'

He still had the bruises, darker now, a yellowish tinge to the skin where he'd been caught on the cheekbone, and a puffiness round one eye. He didn't look like he'd changed either. His T-shirt was still blood-splattered and he smelt of stale blood and fish.

'Shiv gonna mess me up if I don't do what he say,' Pea went on, looking us both up and down. 'Anyways, it all over now, innit.'

'Is it?' said Tokes.

'Sure! Shiv, he jus' need to show you who's boss,' Pea said with a shrug. 'Thanks to me an' da knife trick, he be off your back.'

'So we're supposed to be grateful to you?' I demanded.

'Hey, Hollywood, way I hear it, they cuff Mr T here an' treat you like da Queen.'

'That's not the point,' I said.

'I also hear your mamma pull a few strings to spring you outta jail and leave North London boy to take da rap. Am I right?'

I squirmed because it was true, but Tokes stepped in. 'At least she tried to help which is more than can be said for you.'

'Look, it jus' a bit of fun. No harm done,' said Little Pea.

Tokes shook his head. 'I tried to help you. Twice.'

'I already told you. No point tryin' to save Little Pea, issit!' he said matter-of-factly. 'Social workers. Doctors. Kiddie shrinks. They all say da same. I can't be fixed. I'm a tragic product of a broken society, innit. What can you do?'

'That's just an excuse,' said Tokes. 'So you don't even have to *try* to do the right thing.'

'Hey, you can play da big hero, Mr T. Me, I jus' tryin' to stay alive here.'

Tokes tutted. 'Just remind me never to try and do you a favour again.'

'Chillax, peeps!' Pea said. 'I knows da score. Bas-ic-ally, I owes you one now, innit. An' that is mighty good news for you both today, I'm a-tellin' you!'

'Why?' Tokes growled.

'Cos I gonna make it up to you in style,' said Pea.

'Um, how exactly?' I said.

Pea gave me a giant grin and wiggled his fingers like he was about to do a magic spell. 'Lucky for you today ain't no ordinary day, right? It all goin' down in Coronation Road later.' He nodded towards the window with the view down the High Street. 'And Little Pea can get you in.'

'In on what?' asked Tokes.

'On da action!' Pea said. 'Shiv got stuff planned an' I can tell you da low-down.'

'Why would we want that?' I said.

'Cos we gonna re-claim da streets!' Pea sounded like an excited little kid spouting grown-up ideas. 'Give da po-lice hell for what they done to Pats. It's gonna be da best night Coronation Road has ever seen.'

Tokes just shook his head and said, 'Count me out.'

'We can get us all some good stash!' Pea went on excitedly. 'I got me a shoppin' list right here,' he said, tapping his head. 'Gonna get me new treads, new threads, new phone . . .'

'Don't be stupid, Pea,' said Tokes in a low voice.

'Hey!' said Pea, not bothering to keep his voice down. 'I done da numbers. Too many rioters, not enough police. It's gonna be like taking candy from a baby.'

'And if you get caught you could end up in jail,' I pointed out.

'Not me,' said Pea. 'I'm small. Slip in and outta cracks. Nobody gonna catch me. Hey, I reckon your boyfrien' in da 'lectrical store bes' make sure he locked down his shop pretty tight, eh, Hollywood?'

Pea flicked a glance at Tokes then back at me when he used the word 'boyfriend' and I flushed hotly.

'What are you talking about?' I managed to say.

'I sayin' you totes got da hots for Mr Cricket Captain in da camera shop, innit,' Pea said, eyes flickering from me to Tokes again with a mischievous sparkle. 'I seen you all flutterin' your eyelashes when you go in there.'

'I do not!' I said hotly.

'Whatevs!' Pea giggled. 'That store gonna be a prime target today so bes' have a word wit' lover boy.'

'He's not my boyfriend,' I insisted. 'And I don't fancy him. I hardly even know him!'

Pea just giggled.

'Look, this is totally stupid,' Tokes said quietly, avoiding my eye.

'No ways!' Pea grinned. Then he turned to me and said, 'It be a smokin'-hot endin' to your film too. The neighbourhood on fire, it all kickin' off. It win you an Oscar, I bet!'

But I wasn't really listening any more. I was thinking about what he'd said about the Choudharys' shop, and Tokes's face when he'd mentioned Ishmael. I glanced out of the window again. The crowd seemed to be swaying now, like some giant black jellyfish, pulling and pushing towards the police station. I flicked on my camera and started filming it, but it all seemed weirdly far away, cut off on the other side of the blue glass, like another world.

'So you want in or what?' asked Pea.

I opened my mouth to answer.

'No!' said Tokes firmly. 'We don't.'

'Suit yourself, boy! Why not let Hollywood speak for herself?'

The librarian looked up again and shushed loudly.

'This is a one-time offer, lady!' said Pea, lowering his voice and doing one of his skips.

Off-screen, you can hear Tokes saying, 'She's not

interested.' But he had this look on his face, like he knew what was going to happen; like he knew he couldn't stop it, even though he was going to try.

Pea dragged us over to the Cookery section where he said we could get the best views. With his nose pressed up against the glass, he explained that his assignment was to keep watch from up here and report back to Shiv. He said we had to help out by reporting anything suspicious we spotted. He spent half his time messaging updates on his sparkly pink phone. Every couple of minutes it would beep and he'd start tapping away again.

'Did you even go home last night?' asked Tokes, taking in Pea's crumpled appearance and the dried blood round his face.

'Cuttn't, could I,' he said with a shrug. 'My mamma, she been watchin' da news. She say she gonna lock me in a cupboard or tie me up if she got to, so's I don't get in trouble. She don't trust me that woman.'

'Sounds like my mum!' I muttered.

Pea turned on me then with a look in his eyes that I hadn't seen before. 'Your mamma ever lock you in a cupboard?' he said. 'Or set her boyfrien' on you wit' a belt? Stub out her cigarettes on you like an ashtray, then say you deserve it all cos you da spawn of Satan himself?'

I couldn't tell if he was being serious or not. 'You have no idea what my mum's like,' I blurted out.

'Actually, I do,' said Pea. 'She lyin' politician scum. I seen da film, remember.'

I glanced quickly at Tokes who was staring at me with this questioning expression on his face which made me wish I'd just told him everything in the first place.

'The stuff I filmed, of my mum on the phone the other night . . .' I tried to explain. 'She was talking about Pats. It – it doesn't make her look very good.'

'Make it look like she coverin' up for da po-lice is what she sayin',' Pea added helpfully.

'She never actually comes out and says that,' I replied quickly, surprised to find myself defending her. 'But I suppose it kind of makes it sound that way.'

'Ain't dat da truth, sista,' said Pea.

'I'm sorry I didn't tell you,' I said, turning to Tokes. 'I . . .'

'You just wanted to protect your mum, that's all,' said Tokes.

I shook my head, my face still hot, a tight throbbing behind my eyes again. 'I don't know why. She doesn't deserve it.'

I turned to stare out of the window, blinking hard to stop the tears from coming. For some reason Tokes being nice about it made me feel madder at my mum than ever.

It was still light outside, but the yellow bulbs inside the library and the blue glass made the streets seem a weird sea-green. In the distance I could hear more police sirens. I pressed myself against the window and scanned my camera across the scene.

'I think something's happening,' I said. 'But I can't see properly.'

'What?' asked Pea, jumping up. He pulled a pair of ancient binoculars out of his pocket and I wondered where on earth he'd got them from.

'It's startin',' he squeaked excitedly. 'Curtain jus' about to go up on this show!'

Then he was texting away, quicker than ever. 'Messagin' my intel to da troops,' he said with a broad grin.

'The crowd's moving,' Tokes said. He was beside me now, a shocked expression in his eyes as he stared down. 'It looks like they're trying to break into the police station.'

'I wish we could get a closer look,' I said. The picture was distorted through the coloured glass. I couldn't get a decent shot.

'Maggie, we're not going out there,' said Tokes.

Pea's phone beeped. 'I just got my orders. I know where Shiv headin'!' said Pea excitedly. 'You comin'?'

We both turned to stare at him.

'Look, I tryin' to make up for what happen yesterday, but if you don't want in . . .'

'We could just film it,' I said, turning to Tokes, my heart racing, a picture of my mum telling me to keep out of trouble flickering through my brain. 'We'd just be bystanders. We won't be doing anything wrong.'

'Maggie . . .' said Tokes.

'We'd be invisible,' I said.

'Is that what you reckon?' he said. 'When you've got your camera, no one can see you?'

Just then a spark of orange flared in the air, and we heard something through the thick dark glass – an explosion, followed by yelling, shouting. Was that a gunshot?

The crowd was surging down the High Street now, a dark mass, like a river bursting its banks.

'OMG! They set a bus on fire!' said Little Pea, jittery with excitement.

I stared down at the road below. Sure enough, flames were shooting out of the top windows of a red double-decker bus. People were pouring out of the doors. It was like watching a silent movie, happening in real time, in vivid technicolour.

'This totally rocks!' Little Pea was saying.

It's blurry and tinged with colour, but I have it all on film. The bus in flames. The crowd surging towards it. A wave of policemen running beside the flickering of emergency vehicles and a long strobe light from the helicopter above – like a spotlight on a giant stage show, a circus of madness and fear.

'What's happening?' I said, frightened suddenly.

'The police are pushin' them back,' squeaked Pea. 'Look.'

I looked where he was pointing and could see a line of police with plastic shields pushing the crowd back along the High Street, in our direction.

'It comin' this way!' yelped Pea. 'It time to join da party, peeps!'

SCENE 19: CORONATION ROAD. DUSK

Pea half ran, half fell down the stairs of the library and out into the concrete square.

Tokes followed him at a run, trying to tug him back. But Pea was dancing like he was on hot coals as we burst out into the dusk and our heads were suddenly flooded by sound, light, colour. There was a smell of smoke in the air, the noise of sirens and shouting and smashing glass.

'Gotta split, bluds!' shouted Pea. 'You comin' or what?'

More and more hooded figures were appearing as if from nowhere. It felt like Halloween, or a night at the funfair, only wilder, crazier. It was exciting, weirdly beautiful, terrifying.

Across the street, the window of the newsagent's had been smashed and there were people climbing through the broken glass and tugging stuff out of the display. Further up the road a bin had been set on fire, and the old tramp we'd seen earlier was doing a sort of jig and yelling, 'Death to the Queen!'

I had my camera running by now. The light was fading fast, but I filmed a group of kids outside the sports store, tugging and kicking at the grille, yelling, screaming. They all had their hoods up and some even had scarves tied round their heads so you couldn't make their faces out.

Tokes was glancing up nervously at the CCTV cameras dotted along the street. 'Don't be an idiot, Pea,' you can just hear him say.

'What else I gonna do?' Pea shouted above the roar of sound. 'I ain't exactly gonna be a brain surgeon, issit. My mamma always say I turn bad so I just fulfillin' my destiny.'

'That's the stupidest thing I ever heard,' said Tokes.

But Pea wasn't listening. He pulled up his hood, tugged a scarf round his face and said in a muffled voice, 'Ready for lift-off!' Then he did a little salute before legging it in the direction of the burning bus – a tiny hooded figure silhouetted by the rising flames.

'Should we follow him?' I said.

'No!' Tokes answered, almost yelling. He was staring after Pea, disappointment etched on his face. 'He's made his choice. Come on, let's get away from here.'

'But I need to film this!'

'Why?' he said, turning to look at me. He looked genuinely confused.

And I didn't really have an answer. I think I told myself at the time it was because I was a film-maker, following a story, but maybe it was really because of my mum, because of all the ways it felt like she'd let me down.

'Because . . . because it's the end of the film,' I said at last.

'Maggie, I can't be here when the police come!' said Tokes, his voice cracking with panic. 'And you know I'm not leaving without you.'

I hesitated just for a second. A shout went up as the kids broke down the grille at the sports store. Tokes was looking at me with a pleading expression on his face and I couldn't help thinking of his mum, stroking his cheek, telling him to make her proud.

'OK,' I said. 'Let's go.'

But when we turned round we found the doors to the library had been locked and there was no way of getting back in.

'No!' Tokes kicked the door in frustration. 'We should never have followed that kid.'

'Where now?' I said, nervous suddenly as a loud explosion went off close by.

Tokes hesitated for a second. I think he was frightened too, but trying not to show it. 'My place,' he said, reaching a hand out to me. 'Come on.'

So I took his hand and we both ran.

We made it out of the square and on to the High Street, but the way back was blocked. Hooded figures surged down from the bus station, followed by a line of police with plastic shields.

'Too late!' said Tokes, pulling me into a shop doorway. His face was screwed up with frustration and fear.

I glanced back in the direction we'd come. People had started throwing stuff at the police – bricks, it looked like, and bottles filled with fire that exploded on impact. A car had been set alight further down the road. Smoke and orange flames spilled out from the windows and lapped under the tyres, and the smell was awful – like death in the night. It made my eyes water and my throat gag.

'Come on!' said Tokes, tugging my hand and pulling me back in the direction we'd come from.

'Where are we going now?'

'I don't know,' said Tokes. 'We just need to get away from here.'

So we ran up Coronation Road, past Primark and Iceland and the Ghanaian grocer's, hand in hand, our breath coming in hot, frightened bursts.

Then suddenly a crowd of people charged out from a side street, running from a line of police who were following them with plastic shields. It hit us like a wave, hooded figures pushing, shoving, yelling – anger visible in the eyes of some, laughter in others. I tried to keep hold of Tokes's hand as the crowd pushed us backwards, but then someone was shoving me and I tripped and that was when I felt his fingers wrenched from mine and I was down on the ground and nobody was stopping to help me.

I managed to get up, but I couldn't see Tokes any more. He'd been tugged off by the wave of the crowd who had turned and were now surging back towards the line of police. I stumbled on in the opposite direction, calling out his name, not even knowing which way he'd gone. I was suddenly alone and I was so scared.

And then I saw that I was across the road from Choudhary's Electrical Store. The shutters were down and the TVs inside the window were blank and silent. And then I saw him, by the front doorway: Ishmael Choudhary, looking around nervously, holding a cricket bat.

I stopped. An image flashed into my head of the photo on the mantelpiece at the Choudharys' house, of Ishmael in his cricket whites, hitting a ball for the boundary.

I wanted to shout at him to run away, that the rioters would smash up the shop. That they'd smash *him* up too if he stood in their way.

But he hadn't seen me in the dark and crowded street. I looked at Ishmael, his beautiful features lit up golden in the light from the street lamp. Then the sound of screaming and smashed glass shattered the air and my stomach contracted with fear.

That's when I heard Tokes calling my name and I turned

and saw him emerge from a back alley, hand outstretched. ‘Maggie. Come on!’ he yelled. He didn’t seem to have seen Ishmael. He just wanted to get us both out of there as quickly as possible.

A huge explosion went up from somewhere nearby and fear convulsed through me. We needed to get out of there and I figured I’d got Tokes into enough trouble already, I couldn’t let him down now.

Ishmael had caught sight of me, a look of surprise registering on his face. My mouth felt dry suddenly, with shame and fear, as I stared back.

‘Run!’ was all I managed to say, the words coming out quiet and brittle so I don’t even know if he heard them. ‘You need to run.’

And then *I* was running towards Tokes who grabbed my hand and tugged me away. As I ran, I glanced back to see Ishmael still staring after me, but I just turned away, my stomach a rock of fear as we legged it further up the road, leaving Ishmael to face the rioters alone.

Finally, Tokes dragged me down the alley next to the bridal shop. We stopped, bent double, trying to catch our breath. From further down the road I could still hear loud cheers, glass smashing and that sound that fire makes – not a crackle, more of a white hum below the sirens. And I could feel the fear pumping through my heart.

'We should be OK here,' panted Tokes. I wasn't sure if he was saying it to reassure me or himself.

I was still thinking about Ishmael. It was getting darker and the street lamps made the shadows fall in odd angles all around us. Had the rioters reached the shop yet? What would he do if they tried to break in? I didn't think his bat would be much use against the crowd.

Tokes clambered up on to a wheelie bin to try and get a better view.

'What's happening?' I asked. What I *wanted* to ask was, 'Is Ishmael OK?' But I didn't.

Tokes reached down a hand to pull me up, and before I knew it I was standing next to him. He didn't let go of my hand and I could smell the sharp odour of his sweat. It smelt like fear.

We didn't have a great view, but we could see a small stretch of Coronation Road, not as far down as Choudhary's though so I had no idea if Ishmael was still there. I could see that the front of a furniture shop had been smashed in. A tall man was staggering down the road carrying a leather armchair, and a gang of kids was dancing along with fancy lamps in their hands, singing loudly.

My phone vibrated in my pocket – it had been buzzing all the time we'd been running – and when I pulled it out there were three missed calls and six text messages from my mum.

WHERE ARE YOU? said one. I couldn't tell from the bare syllables whether she was worried or mad at me.

AT LIBRARY I texted back, one-handed, the fingers of my other hand still entwined with Tokes's.

STAY WHERE YOU ARE the text came back almost immediately. DO NOT GO OUTSIDE.

'See, she's worried about you,' said Tokes, who had been peering over my shoulder.

I shook my head. 'She just doesn't want me to make her look bad.' My voice came out a bit shaky so I coughed to try and steady it. 'What about your mum? You want to let her know you're OK?'

He nodded and I handed him my phone. He let go of my hand as he typed quickly into it then waited for it to beep a reply.

'Is she all right?'

'She's fine. She says she'll stay at work till it's over.' Then he hesitated. 'Maybe I could . . .' He stopped.

'What?'

'Nah,' he shook his head and handed me back the phone. 'I thought maybe I could send my dad a text, but he doesn't even know I'm here, so I guess he won't be worried about me.'

I frowned. I didn't want to think about whether my dad was worried about me so I switched my camera back on, focusing on the bit of Coronation Road that was visible. There was a group of girls running along in massive multicoloured wigs, carrying bulging bags, laughing like they were at a fairground.

'Do you reckon you'll ever see him again?' I asked.

'My dad?'

I nodded. It was weird having this conversation on a wheelie bin with the streets burning around us, but I felt as if I needed to talk, to fill the air with words and keep the fear at bay.

'I know he'll find us sooner or later,' Tokes was saying. 'But my mum says she'll only take him back if he drops out of the gang.' He stopped. 'And I don't think he can.'

There was a huge crash from just beyond the alley and I saw somebody had started a fire inside the furniture shop. A sofa was burning, fingers of orange flame starting to lick out of the window. I thought of the Choudharys' shop, the TVs on display, the Special Offer signs in Mr Choudhary's curling handwriting.

'Why?' I said quickly, pushing the thought out of my brain. 'Why can't he just give it all up?'

'Cos you don't just drop out of a gang and live to tell the tale.' Tokes kept staring ahead and I got the feeling he needed to keep talking too, that he was as scared as I was. 'And, even if he could, he's got a criminal record. No education. No skills. How's he gonna live? Who's gonna give him a job?'

A loud police siren punctuated the air, accompanied by screams and laughter. Tokes looked down at me, his eyes reflecting the lick of the flames in the sky. 'What about your mum and dad?' he asked then. 'You think they'll get back together?'

I shook my head. 'Sometimes it feels like he left me when he left her. Like he divorced us both.'

I don't think I'd really admitted that to myself before, that my brilliant dad had let me down. I felt myself wobbling on the wheelie bin and Tokes put his arm round me to hold me steady. I could feel his hand on my shoulder and the warmth of his skin against mine.

'He sends you doughnuts every week,' he said.

'I'm sick of doughnuts!' I looked down at my feet. The Tippex faces were covered in white dust. Only the eyes were visible, but they were blank, unreadable. 'I'd rather talk to him. See him.'

I shivered and Tokes pulled me a bit closer. I looked up. Our faces were centimetres apart now. His eyes flickered down to my chapped lips then back to my eyes, and he seemed about to say something, but just then there was a huge crash, louder and closer than before, and a load of shouting. People had started pouring out of the furniture store like insects, scrambling into a run as the flames licked higher and higher.

That was when I saw the line of riot police with plastic shields running down the road. I zoomed my camera in as close as I could, but it was nearly dark and the images were fuzzy.

'Are you scared?' I asked, looking up at Tokes to see myself reflected in his eyes. My hair looked red in the orange light, spiky like the flames.

'A bit,' he said. 'You?'

I nodded my head.

Just then my phone beeped. I tugged it out of my pocket and looked at the message on the screen. **HELP HURT BAD CUM QUICK.**

'Who's it from?'

At the end was a single consonant – not in capital letters. **p**.

Tokes groaned loudly and jumped down off the wheelie bin. 'This is another of his tricks,' he said.

I looked towards Coronation Road again. The police had pushed the rioters further up, past Primark. I imagined Pea lying hurt somewhere, all alone.

'What if it's for real this time?' I said.

Tokes shook his head and let out a hissing sound through his teeth. 'I don't care. I'm not falling for it again. Every time I do something nice for that kid he lands me in trouble.'

'But what if he's really hurt?'

Tokes closed his eyes tightly. 'Maggie, I *can't*. He had his chance.'

His face was sort of twisted in pain and he sounded like he was trying to convince us both.

I stared down at the message from Pea. I filmed it too, focusing my camera on the sad, bare syllables.

WHERE ARE YOU? I texted back.

ICELAND came back the reply, fast as lightning. POLISMAN GOT ME WITH HIS BATON BLUD EVERYWHERE LIKE HORROR FILM.

I looked up. Tokes was pacing the alley, his eyes staring but unseeing.

'A policeman hit him,' I said.

Tokes kicked the wall, so hard it must have really hurt. He grimaced then did it again. 'I don't believe this!' he muttered. 'Why us? Why is he texting us?'

'Cos it's like you said – we're the only friends he has. The only ones who might actually help him anyway.' I started clambering down off the bin. My camera was still rolling. I don't know why I didn't switch it off. I guess I wanted it to be ready . . . just in case.

The phone beeped again. This time the message said simply, PLEES.

'I'll go,' I said.

I don't know why I said it. Whether I really wanted to help Pea, be a hero. Maybe I did it to annoy my mum, or because my dad hadn't bothered to text for days. Or to stop Tokes going. I don't know, but once I'd said it I knew there was no going back.

'No!' groaned Tokes. 'You can't. It's too dangerous.'

'He's hurt.'

'So he says!' said Tokes, looking up at me desperately. 'Maggie, remember what happened yesterday. Think what your mum will say.'

Maybe that was what made my mind up. It was like, when he mentioned my mum, something in my brain flipped. 'I don't care!' I said, pushing his hand away. 'I don't care about her. I don't care about getting into trouble. I'm going.'

He stared at me like he almost didn't recognise me for a moment. Then he shook his head and said, 'Well, you can't go on your own.'

'Yes, I can,' I said quickly. It was my fault Tokes was even out there in the first place; there was no way I was dragging him into even more trouble. 'Anyway, it's less dangerous for me than it is for you.'

'How do you figure that?' he asked.

'Because you're already on a caution.'

Tokes glanced up at the sky for a second, his jaw tense with frustration.

'You don't need to look after me,' I said.

'I know.' He looked down and his eyes met mine again.

'And I'm only going to run round to Iceland and check if he's even there,' I insisted. 'If I need your help, I'll come back and get you.' I was lying and I think he knew it, but I was determined to keep him safe this time.

Tokes stared right back at me. He opened his mouth to argue with me, but I cut him off.

'I don't need your permission,' I said firmly, almost angrily, because I had to protect him and this was the only way I could think to do it, even if I hurt him in the process.

A pained expression crossed his face. 'I know that. I'm just saying . . .'

'Well, don't,' I snapped, unable to meet his eye. 'Stop telling me what I can and can't do.'

He tried to put his hand on my arm again and I yanked it away. 'Just get off me, will you?' I yelled. It felt horrible, treating him like this, but it was the only way. 'I'm going and don't you dare try to stop me.'

And then I was running, away from Tokes, out of the alleyway in the direction of Coronation Road. Fear was pumping through me so hard I could hardly feel my legs.

And suddenly I was out there, in front of the blazing furniture store. The heat hit me like a boiling wave and the thick, acrid black smoke stung my eyes so I could hardly see where I was going. Everything seemed different suddenly and I was confused by the smoke and the sound of screaming and the adrenalin dancing in my brain. I stumbled forward, tears streaming down my cheeks, trying to remember which way Iceland was, and then I crashed into an upturned bin and landed face down on the pavement. I must have cut my hand on something – glass or a shard of metal – because I felt a hot trickle of blood running down my wrist and a sharp stab of something like pain that seemed weirdly far away.

And then a pair of hands was pulling me to my feet and a familiar voice was saying, 'I don't care what you say. We're safer if we stick together,' and that was when the pain hit me, because I hadn't managed to keep Tokes safe after all. He'd followed me.

SCENE 20: CORONATION ROAD. EVENING

The flames from the fire in the furniture store were two storeys high now, making the air all around flicker and tremble. The line of police had pushed up beyond the station towards the common, but there were still bunches of people hanging out in shop doorways, climbing over cars, kicking at bins. As we approached Iceland, we saw people with loaded shopping bags. One woman was pushing a trolley piled high with frozen-food boxes.

'Can you see him?' I asked.

Tokes shook his head. 'If this is another set-up, I'm gonna kill him myself!'

We circled past the shop and up the side street it backed on to. Huge industrial dustbins and cardboard boxes were scattered across the alleyway, but there was no sign of Pea.

'Let's check under the arches behind Iceland,' Tokes said, nodding towards the train-station entrance where the two policemen had stopped us the day before.

'You should go back,' I said for what felt like the millionth time. My voice was hoarse from the smoke fumes and I wasn't even sure I meant what I was saying any more.

'Will you stop it, Maggie? I'm not leaving you out here on your own, no matter how much you yell at me,' he replied. 'Come on.'

He made his way towards the train station and I followed him, knowing there was no point arguing. The shutters were down and there was a big notice saying *Police Incident – Station Closed*. It seemed desolate without the usual rush of evening commuters. Pea wasn't there.

'He's playing us again,' Tokes said with a sigh. 'Come on. Let's get out of here.'

But then, just as we were coming back out on to the alley, we saw him, curled up in a ball, tucked so tightly into the shadow of the wall that we nearly missed him.

'Pea!' I called.

He looked up. There was fresh blood on the side of his head, matted into his hair. In the dim light it glowed sticky and wet.

Tokes was by his side in a couple of strides. 'What happened?'

Pea looked relieved for a second, pleased to see us, like he hadn't expected us to come. 'Got clobbered by a policeman, dittn't I?' he said, looking round with a nervous grin on his face. I wondered then if he ever stopped smiling. He smiled when he was scared, when he was angry, when he was guilty, like it was the only expression he knew.

'Really?' Tokes looked doubtful.

'True as!' Pea insisted. 'Comin' outta SportsMad wit' a loada gear an' they grab me. Reckon I smash one copper round da head wit' a hockey stick, only then a loada them come at me wit' those batons.' I stared at him, trying to work out if he was telling the truth. 'Police brutality that is – like what happened to Pats,' he went on. 'I gonna get them sued, I reckon.'

'Not if you get yourself killed first,' said Tokes. 'Come on, we'll take you home.'

He tugged Pea up, like he was light as a feather, put an arm under his shoulder and started half carrying, half tugging him back up the road, away from the trouble.

'Don't wanna go home,' said Pea defiantly, wriggling to try and get free. 'My mamma'll batter me so much worse'n da feds if she see me wit' all this.' He pointed to the massive rucksack he still had attached to his back, bulging with stuff.

'Have you seriously been nicking stuff?' asked Tokes, shaking his head, but not letting go of Pea.

'What did I tell you? Been like a supermarket sweep out there!'

'Then you need to get out of here before the police arrest you,' said Tokes, tugging him even harder than before. We could hear the sirens overhead, the yelling of the riot police further up the road. We were getting closer to Mr Choudhary's shop and a sick feeling rose in my throat. Was Ishmael still there? Was he OK?

'No way. I ain't finished my Christmas shoppin' yet,' Pea was saying.

Tokes stopped and turned to look at him, his face wild, frustrated. 'Why did you text us if you don't even want us to help you?' His hood had fallen down and you could see him clearly in the light of the street lamp.

'Cos you gotta film this!' announced Pea, grabbing my camera out of my hand and clicking it on to record mode before shoving it back in my hand. 'Check it out!' He was pointing down the road and now I could see what he was going on about. There was a crowd gathered outside Choudhary's Electrical Store, pushing, jeering, shouting.

'Word on da street is your boyfrien' has gone all vigilante,' Pea said gleefully, grinning at me.

'What?' My stomach leapt violently.

'Shop boy's takin' on da mob!' said Pea, waving an arm in the direction of Choudhary's. 'Blood gonna be shed, I tellin' you!'

That was when I saw Ishmael. The crowd of hooded figures had him surrounded. They were jostling him, shaking the mesh wiring, yelling. He was still holding the cricket bat in his hand and I could just about hear him saying, 'This is a family business. Go home. Leave this shop alone.' His voice was calm and measured.

'What is he doing?' said Tokes.

The crowd was pushing Ishmael backwards, laughing at him. Some of them were tugging at the metal grille, trying to heave it up.

I felt sick. My camera was in my hand and I'd filmed him saying that, sounding more like a Bollywood star than ever.

'Good or what?' said Little Pea, grinning widely.

'He's gonna . . .' Tokes was staring. 'He must be mad.'

'You are stealing from your own people – your own community!' Ishmael was saying, louder now. But the crowd wasn't listening. They were grabbing at his clothes, more aggressive every second. And I stood there, rooted to the spot, too shocked even to realise that I was still filming.

'We should do something,' I heard myself whisper.

'Nuttin' we can do,' said Pea. 'He got a death wish ob-vi-ous-ly!'

'But we can't just . . .'

Then one voice soared above the noise of the crowd, yelling, 'Get out the way or we gon' slash your face, boy.'

'Shiv!' squeaked Pea.

I felt my heart sink.

‘Oh man!’ said Pea. ‘This jus’ get better an’ better!’

I could see Shiv now. Right at the front of the crowd, his eyes glowing a weird yellowy-orange in the light of the street lamp. And in his hand something flashed – the sharp flicker of a blade. He was waving it around in front of Ishmael like a snake charmer. The rest of the crowd had drawn back, away from the shining arc of the knife.

At my side I could hear Tokes’s breathing quicken. ‘Come on!’ he said, pulling Pea by the arm and not even looking at me. ‘There’s nothing we can do. We need to get out of here.’

‘We can’t just leave him!’ I said, my head spinning with confusion and panic. ‘I know him.’

Tokes turned to look at me. He’d reached out his hand to take mine, but I was frozen, holding my camera, not knowing what to do. It was my fault Tokes was there, and I’d promised myself I’d keep him safe, but I couldn’t just turn my back on Ishmael for a second time.

Ishmael was facing Shiv, gripping his bat tightly. I could see his face more clearly now that the crowd had drawn back a little. He had a look of intense concentration, his eyes following the flickering blade as it danced before him.

‘Step back or I will use this. I’m warning you!’ he said, wielding the bat, his voice calm.

I watched in horror as Shiv laughed and took another step

forward. The crowd shifted and I couldn't see Ishmael's face properly any more.

'Shop boy is a total headcase!' said Pea with a high-pitched giggle. 'Shiv gonna slash him if he don' step aside.'

I felt a jolt of nausea race through me because I knew Pea was right.

'Please, Tokes,' I said. 'We need to do something.'

'There's nothing we can do,' said Tokes, but he still didn't move and when I glanced at him he looked torn, like he suddenly didn't know what to do either. He looked a bit like he had in the park, that first day, when he'd seen Shiv torturing Pea. Like he knew walking away was no longer an option for him.

'I say again, this is a family business. Please leave,' Ishmael called out. 'We have no argument with you, but I will fight to defend our property.'

'Get – out – of – my – way,' hissed Shiv. I could only see the back of his black hood now, and the bright flicker of his blade.

Everything seemed to be happening really quickly. The film loop was running away with me. Ishmael raised his bat, Shiv stepped closer with the knife, the crowd surged forward. Little Pea just stood there, staring. Tokes's face was set in grim determination, his fists balled.

'They're going to hurt him . . .' I said, turning to Tokes.

The crowd was roaring like a pack of animals, tearing at the grille, throwing bricks. And I couldn't see Ishmael or Shiv now, but I could hear a scream that sounded like Ishmael.

And suddenly I was rushing forward. I don't know what I thought I was going to do, how I was going to stop Shiv or save Ishmael, but I just knew I had to try.

'Maggie! What are you doing? Stop!'

I felt Tokes dragging me backwards.

'I've got to help him!' I was yelling, trying to pull away from Tokes, but he was stronger than me and he swung me round to face him, his hands clasping my arms in an iron grip.

'No, Maggie! We can't get involved in this!' he was saying, his face close to mine.

'He's my friend,' I half sobbed, half stammered. 'I – I should have warned him. If he gets hurt, it's my fault.'

We were metres away from Ishmael now. Shiv was waving the knife in his face, but he was still refusing to step aside. Tokes looked back at me. His eyes were staring, but it was like he wasn't really seeing me, or seeing anything, like there was some kind of struggle going on in his head, more intense even than the fight that was happening in front of us.

Then he let out a deep groan and shook his head. 'I am a total idiot!' he muttered. And he let go of my arms and started running from my side, across the street, and the next thing I saw he was pulling at Shiv, trying to drag him away from Ishmael. His hood was down and in the light of the street lamp I caught a flash of his face and it was wild, desperate, gutted.

'This is like da best action movie ever!' shrieked Pea, dancing up and down, more excited than I'd ever seen him.

But I felt almost numb with terror. I was dimly aware of the camera in my hand, still filming as everything happened with terrifying speed before my eyes.

Then suddenly I heard a wild roar, a scream of pain more raw and desperate than anything before.

A shout went up as the crowd managed to yank the shutters open. A brick was thrown, smashing the window. People surged into the shop.

'He's been stabbed!' I heard someone yell. 'Call 999.'

My heart was pounding so fast now I could hear it in my ears like the rush of the ocean, drowning me. I could hardly work out what was happening on-screen or off. My camera was shaking in my hand, but I kept filming, frozen to the spot. I'd filmed it all. It was as if that was all I was capable of doing . . . like I couldn't stop even if I wanted to.

Beside me, Pea was jumping up and down, his eyes round as saucers.

'Who's hurt?' I heard myself whisper.

'He's bleeding!' I heard someone cry.

'Who?' I couldn't figure out anything any more. The scream came in short bursts and the shouts of the crowd were louder than ever.

Someone yelled, 'There's blood everywhere!'

'Who? Whose blood is it?' I couldn't see Tokes or Ishmael through the blur of bodies and panic was rising through me faster and faster and I could hardly breathe.

Another voice – maybe mine. 'Someone needs to call an ambulance.'

Then Pea grabbed my hand and sent my camera flying.

'You gotta run,' he squealed, yanking me by the shoulders and yelling in my face, so close I could see right into his rose-pink mouth, see the staring whites of his frightened eyes. 'Get outta here and take North London boy wit' you.'

'What?' I was lost in panic and now it all seemed to be happening in a fog. My camera had gone flying through the air. I'd seen it spin off in an arc through the flame-lit sky. Saw it land with a crash on the pavement and a foot stamp it to the ground.

I heard myself yell something, I don't know what. I felt like I was underwater, unable to think properly. And for some reason all I was able to focus on was my camera. Maybe because, more than ever before, I wanted to hide behind it and watch what was happening as if it was a movie, not real life. Like maybe I could press rewind and Tokes and Ishmael would both be OK.

I pulled away from Pea and flung myself forward, scrabbling on the ground, trying to rescue my camera from the stampede of black-hooded figures who were pushing their way into the shop.

'Forget that!' yelled Pea, trying to pull me away. 'You gotta get him outta here 'fore da feds come.'

Just at that moment I felt the camera under my palm. I picked it up. The viewfinder was smashed and when I pressed the 'on' button nothing happened. I remember staring at it, panic filling me, expanding within my head like water in a balloon. It felt as if the world was unravelling, like the broken camera was the end of everything.

Pea was still tugging at me. He pulled me to my feet till I was looking at him, and he yelled, 'Shop boy been stabbed. You get that? Now you need to stop Tokes bein' a hero or he get hisself killed too. Look!'

He pushed my head round and I saw Ishmael lying on the floor by the entrance to his father's shop, a dark stain of blood spreading out all around him. Pieces of his cricket bat were by his side. Tokes was bending over him, covered in blood, his hand pressed on to a place that oozed red, thick and fast.

I felt as if I was going to be sick, or pass out.

'Call 999!' I heard Tokes yell out to the crowd of figures swarming round the shop. 'Someone! Please!'

'You need to get him outta here,' Pea was shouting.

But I couldn't move. I couldn't take it all in without the filter of the lens. It was too much.

'I . . .' I stuttered, staring at Pea, frozen in panic.

'Oh, for goodness' sake!' muttered Pea. And then he was gone from my side, and I saw him darting away in the direction of the shop. The crowd had smashed the window and people were tugging stuff out of the display while Ishmael lay bleeding on the pavement. One of the giant TVs was shattered on the road nearby.

And I just knelt there, staring. I remember that there were tears pouring down my face, and that I knew I should be doing something, but I couldn't think what. I was hardly able to remember to keep breathing. And then suddenly Pea was back and he was pressing something into my hand. 'Here. Take this – looks pretty much da same. Now go.'

'What?' I looked down, my brain slow to understand. The whole scene seemed blurry and distorted, as if it was being filmed at the wrong speed. In one hand I was holding my old smashed camera; in the other was a brand-new one, almost identical. Something in me realised that Pea must have nabbed the new one from the shop, from the shelves of cameras Mr Choudhary kept behind the counter.

'I can't take this,' I managed to whisper. 'I . . .'

But Pea wasn't listening. 'You gotta dump your old one

where no one ever find it,' he said. 'You hear me?'

'But I . . .'

He had hold of my shoulders again, so I had to turn and look at him. It seemed funny that he was acting like the grown-up suddenly. I stared at his weird little face. The blood was still glistening in the light of the flames and he wasn't grinning for once – he actually looked serious, his dark button eyes fixed intently on mine. 'Look, Maggie, I tryin' to do a good thing for once in my life. Get rid of it an' get him outta here, OK?'

I nodded numbly as his face broke back into a grin – the same cheeky Pea once more.

'Sorted. Now I gotta split. See ya 'round, peeps!' Then he let go of my shoulders, glanced around quickly and was gone. Disappeared. Just like that.

'Someone call an ambulance,' Tokes was still yelling. I couldn't film that – the bit when he was trying to save Mr Choudhary's son and no one would help him – because my old camera was bust and the new one wasn't charged yet.

Someone near me was yelling that the police were on their way. I heard a voice – it might even have been Pea's – saying, 'A man's been stabbed . . . Choudhary's Electrical Store . . . he's bleeding bad . . .'

Then I heard someone shout, 'Police!' and people started pouring out of the front of the shop and disappearing down side streets, carrying boxes and bags under their arms, scattering stuff as they went. Another TV smashed on to the pavement, glass shattering everywhere.

'Help!' Tokes was saying. 'Maggie, I need you to help!'

I ran my finger over the crushed camera, and I remember thinking that I'd never be able to finish the film now.

'Maggie, come on,' Tokes was yelling at me. 'Help me pick him up!'

Maybe that's why I shoved the stolen camera into my pocket. Because I had this mad idea that I needed it to finish the film, that, if I did, I could make happy endings for everyone. For Tokes. And Pea. And even Ishmael.

Or maybe my mum was right and I didn't know how to look life directly in the eye. It doesn't matter really. The result is the same either way.

'Maggie! Come on!' Tokes screamed and I managed to stumble blindly over to where he was crouched, cradling Ishmael in his arms. Even though I didn't film it, the image is still imprinted on my brain: the blood staining Ishmael's shirt and spilling out on to the pavement as he gasped, his eyes staring up at the helicopters criss-crossing the sky, his eyelids opening and shutting helplessly. Tokes was pressing hard on the place the blood was coming from, but it kept spilling out.

I couldn't believe how much blood there was. Suddenly the whole scene came sharply into focus again, bright, vivid, ringing. I could smell blood and fire in the air, and Tokes's voice was sharp and clear through the sound of the sirens and the yelling of the crowd. 'The fire brigade are up by the furniture store,' he was saying. 'We need to get him up there. They can sort him out.'

My breath was coming hot and fast, and the cut on my hand was suddenly searing with pain. I knew this was all happening because of me, but I felt sick and frightened and all I wanted was to be at home.

'You can't be here,' I muttered.

'Maggie!'

'I'm sorry,' I whispered, looking away, not able to look at Ishmael, at the blood. I was shivering and cold and I felt as if I was going to be sick at any moment. 'This is all my fault.'

'Forget that,' Tokes said, his voice desperate, urgent. 'Help me, Maggie – come on!'

Somebody shouted, 'Cops coming!' and I turned and saw a wall of police advancing, riot shields in front of them like plastic shells.

'The police are coming,' I whispered.

But Tokes didn't even seem to care. His hand was on Ishmael's chest. Ishmael's eyes – his beautiful, black liquid eyes – stared up into Tokes's pebble bright ones. For just a second they flickered in my direction and I felt the familiar jolt in my stomach and then they fluttered back to Tokes before slowly closing. Tokes was talking to him, patting his face, begging him to wake up, but he didn't reopen his eyes.

'We have to go, Tokes,' I said, tears streaming down my face – tears of fear, of shame, of terror. 'Pea says we can't be here.'

The policemen were shouting and advancing, only about a hundred metres away now. I stared at Ishmael again and I could taste Mrs Choudhary's honey cake, mixed with the tinny smell of blood on my lips. I remembered the way he would always smile politely at me when I came in the shop, the way he shook my hand on the steps of our house.

'We can't just leave him,' Tokes was saying. He was looking up at me now, his face full of fear and disbelief, and I could see that he was crying too.

I stared at him, my heart racing. All I wanted to do was run away, but I needed him to come too. I couldn't leave him here. 'Tokes, I . . .'

But he had closed his eyes and was shaking his head. 'You go,' he was saying. 'Get out of here. I'll stay.'

'No, I . . . you said . . . we need to stick together.'

He looked up then, held my eye. He looked disappointed, scared but something else too, something steely and determined. 'You promised you'd go if I told you to.' He stared hard at me and he said again, 'Now go, Maggie.'

I stood there for a second. I remembered his fingers locked

round mine, his eyes straying to my lips then back up to my eyes. And my heart twisted in pain that I thought would bleed red all over the pavement and never stop.

Then I turned and ran.

SCENE 21: CORONATION ROAD. THE NEXT DAY

It was blisteringly hot the next morning. The heatwave wasn't stopping for anything, although the sky was clouded, holding in the heat like a blanket, pressing it down on the city.

On Coronation Road, half the shops were open as usual, the other half either boarded up, burned out or smashed to pieces, and yet the sun shone down like it was a holiday.

There was stuff everywhere. Broken glass and ripped clothes and boxes and bottles and bags were strewn all over the road. I saw a single new trainer in the gutter and a load of clothes shoved into an incinerated rubbish bin. A sofa lay on its side outside the kebab shop.

The news crews had descended on Coronation Road too. I stood for ages watching a cameraman as he panned over the scene of destruction. I watched the way he focused in on random items and isolated acts of vandalism, making video bites for the evening news. In my pocket I felt the cracked case of my broken camera and I remembered the footage that was on it. I thought of the other camera, under my bed at home, and I felt sick.

Iceland now had one window boarded up and a crowd of journalists around it. In the middle of them all stood my mum in a petrol-blue suit and a pair of yellow cleaning gloves, holding a broom and talking in a loud voice. A six o'clock news voice.

'This was a flagrant act of lawlessness by people who have no regard for their community.' Her voice was strident but honeyed. 'I assure you that they *will* be brought to justice.' She paused and then insisted, 'They *will* pay for what they have done!'

I didn't need to film her saying that; it would be on every news programme later that day.

She'd said the same thing over breakfast too. That the police would not rest till they had caught everyone involved, every rioter, every looter, everyone who had taken even a penny's worth of goods that were not their own. They would all be caught. I had just stared down at my cereal and said nothing.

'Are you feeling all right?' she'd asked me.

'Fine,' I'd muttered.

'You look peaky. Maybe stay at home and rest today,' she said.

'Fine,' I said again.

'I'd rather you didn't go out anyway. Not even to the library. I dread to think what you could have got yourself caught up in yesterday.'

She didn't ask me if I'd been frightened. If I was OK. If my friends were OK. She'd been too busy running through her speech for the cameras. She was in the work bubble – I could see her through it, but not reach her. I doubt she'd have heard even if I had told her what really happened last night.

'The police are combing through CCTV footage to identify rioters,' she was telling the journalists now. 'And we appeal to parents to help. We ask mums and dads to report their sons and daughters if they suspect they may have been involved.'

I almost laughed when I heard her saying that. But it hurt too, deep in the pit of my stomach.

'In particular we call for witnesses to the stabbing of Ishmael Choudhary to come forward,' she went on. 'Anyone who saw what happened is urged to contact the police immediately.'

Her words echoed round my head. Because I hadn't just witnessed what happened, I'd actually filmed it. My camera might be broken, but the memory card was intact. I knew because after I got home last night I'd watched the footage on the cracked screen, tears running down my face. It was all there, clearer on camera than in real life, especially when I slowed it down and watched it frame by frame. Sometimes it was blurred, or figures got in the way, but it definitely told the true story: Shiv stabbing Ishmael, Tokes trying to stop him, blood bursting out of Ishmael's chest like a rose – even worse on film than it had seemed in real time. I'd replayed it over and over again, as if somehow I'd hoped that the ending might be different. But it never was.

Pea had told me to get rid of the camera. Because he knew what I'd filmed. I had footage that could put Shiv away and Pea didn't want that. He also knew Shiv would come after me if he knew I'd filmed it, let alone handed it to the police. I think Pea thought if I threw it away I'd be safe, safe from Shiv, safe from the Starfish, safe from the police even.

But I couldn't quite bring myself to destroy the camera like Pea had said. Just in case. So I figured I needed to hide it and I could only think of one place. Maybe I was hoping Tokes would be there too. But when I pushed myself through the hole in the fence there was no sign of him.

I stashed the broken camera inside one of the sofa cushions. I pushed it hard so that it was right in the centre of the foam and you didn't even notice if you sat on it. Then I waited, listening to the announcements from the platform above, watching the pigeons flying in and out of the netting. But Tokes didn't come. Nor did Little Pea.

I sat there and the images from the night before came flooding back. I couldn't stop thinking of all the blood, and the expression on Tokes's face when I ran away and left him. I felt like I'd never stop seeing it.

Eventually, I couldn't stand it any more. I needed to know if Ishmael was OK, if Tokes was OK. I needed to find out somehow.

I couldn't face going to Tokes's bedsit and the Choudhary house was empty. So I went to the electrical store. I think I knew I'd end up there eventually. It's always like that in the movies. The main character always goes back to the scene of the crime.

As I got closer, I could see the windows had been boarded up and there was police incident tape cordoning off an area of pavement in front. There were posters on the lamp posts too – a picture of Ishmael in a blue shiny shirt and under it the words, *Witness appeal. A man was stabbed at this location around 7.45 p.m. on the night of the 7th August. If you have any information or witnessed this attack, please contact . . .*

On the floor around the police tape there were already bunches of flowers, like people leave at car-crash sites where someone has died. And messages too: *Get well soon, Ishmael Choudhary* and *Coronation Road Community Centre sends love and prayers to the Choudhary family at this difficult time.*

I took a few steps closer. There was an ugly stain on the pavement, the colour of barbecue sauce. It was even bigger than I remembered, and brighter too in the glare of the summer sun.

Suddenly I didn't want to be there any more. I glanced up at the CCTV camera on the building opposite and remembered Tokes saying, 'You think no one can see you?'

That was when I noticed that the door of the store was open and Mr Choudhary was standing in front of the counter, surrounded by debris. He was motionless, staring at nothing. But he looked up suddenly and saw me, hovering just outside the doorway.

'Ah, Miss Maggie,' he said. He tried to smile, but his face looked like a crinkled piece of paper. His tie, usually so neat, was wonky and his shirt was crumpled. 'Come in, come in. Always welcome, my young friend, even in these . . . dreadful times.'

He waved an arm around as I stepped inside the shop and took in the smashed counter, the shelves torn from the walls, and the cash register wrenched open and thrown through a display cabinet.

'I came to see what they have done to my shop,' Mr Choudhary was saying, his voice hoarse as if he had been shouting or crying. 'These animals – these street rats – you see they have taken everything.'

I thought of the camera hidden under my bed at home and I felt boiling hot with shame.

'How is Ishmael?' I asked quickly, blinking back the tears pressing behind my eyeballs.

Mr Choudhary nodded, but his face was unreadable. 'Yes. I have been all night at the hospital,' he said slowly, as if the words were hard to say. 'He is "holding in there", the doctors tell us. That is my Ishmael. Always good at dropping anchor at the crease. Never one to bow out of a long innings.'

I didn't really understand, but I nodded anyway. 'Is he going to . . . will he be . . . OK?'

'The doctors say it is too early to tell,' said Mr Choudhary with a smile that wasn't a smile really. 'But I know my son. He will not be going back to the pavilion just yet, I think.'

He glanced round the shop again, a smile flitting across his lined face. 'You know, I have five beautiful daughters, but my wife and I are only blessed with one son.' His eyes ran over the counter where Ishmael had stood beside him, day after day. 'That does not make him any more precious than the rest, of course, but . . .'

He hesitated, appeared to be thinking for a moment. 'You know, I was remembering just now, before you came in, about the time he started playing hard-ball cricket. He was young – nine I think – and very small and scrappy.'

I tried to imagine a nine-year-old Ishmael, skinny like Pea, but still with those intense eyes which had sparked with anger last night then seemed suddenly to lose their light.

'I took him to the sports store to get him kitted out,' Mr Choudhary went on, still smiling. 'Proper whites, pads, box, helmet – a real little English cricketer!' He chuckled at the memory. 'I remember thinking that I wanted him to be safe, that nothing would be allowed to hurt my son, my beloved boy . . .'

He tailed off again and I saw there were tears running down his cheeks. Then, to my horror, he put his head in his hands and let out a low sob.

I had no idea what to do. I wanted to turn and run.

'I'm so sorry,' I said hesitantly. 'I . . . I . . .' I'm not sure what I wanted to say, but no words would come out. The shop seemed unbelievably hot and I felt trapped, claustrophobic, like I couldn't breathe. I stood there, watching him cry, watching the sobs wrack his body. And I wanted to tell him about the camera and how I hadn't warned Ishmael and how I'd run away, but I couldn't. I just couldn't.

'My apologies,' he said after a minute, looking up with a loud sniff. 'Forgive an old man for a moment of weakness.' He tugged a large brightly spotted handkerchief out of his pocket and blew his nose noisily, then smiled brightly and said, 'Now I must get on. There is much to be done and this sniffling is not getting the baby bathed, as my wife would say.'

'Do you want some help?' I said. 'Tidying up or anything.'

'No, no, I need to get back to the hospital presently,' he

said with a wave of his handkerchief. 'I just came to pick up a few things from the house, and to see the extent of the damage here.' He paused. 'I have seen it now.'

'I'd better . . . I need to . . . go,' I muttered.

'Thank you for coming, Miss Maggie,' he said, giving one of his formal little bows and holding out his hand to shake mine. 'We are fortunate to have good neighbours like you to remind us that not all our fellow men are like the animals who did this.'

My stomach lurched again as he pressed my hand firmly and smiled through red-rimmed eyes. And I couldn't bear to think how he would look at me if he knew that I was one of those animals who had stolen and stood by and watched while Ishmael was attacked, then run away and left him bleeding on the ground.

When he finally let go of my hand, I half ran, half stumbled out of the shop, blinking back tears as I emerged into the sunshine.

'Is he going to live?'

I spun round and for a second I couldn't see anyone. Then there he was, just a few metres away. Tokes looked pale, like he hadn't slept much or all the blood had run out of him the same way it had out of Ishmael Choudhary. He looked as if something had changed deep inside him and the sunshine had gone out of his smile.

'You're OK?' I said, my heart leaping with happiness to see he was safe, but then sinking again when I remembered how much trouble I'd got him into last night.

'I'm all right.' He shrugged.

I tried to meet his eye, but I couldn't. 'I'm sorry,' I stammered. 'I'm sorry I left you there.'

Tokes gave another shrug. 'You did the right thing.'

He didn't seem mad at me at all and somehow that made it worse.

'It was my fault you were there in the first place,' I said.

But he wasn't listening. He was staring at the half-open door of the shop and tugging me away, further up the street where we couldn't be seen. 'Will he be OK?' he said. 'Ishmael Choudhary I mean.'

I felt myself blush at the mention of his name, even though that seemed silly now, after all that had happened. 'They don't know,' I said.

Tokes sighed. He was looking up at the camera across the road from Mr Choudhary's shop. 'You know, Coronation Road is covered in CCTV,' he said. 'The police will be going through the footage now.'

'You didn't do anything wrong,' I said quickly.

'I didn't hang around when the police got there,' he said quietly. 'I waited till they were close to us so I knew they would help him, then I ran. I should have stayed to give a statement, but I didn't in case they arrested me.'

I glanced up at the CCTV camera further up the street, its lens trained on the spot where the blood patterned the pavement.

'It will all be on CCTV,' I said. 'They'll be able to see it wasn't you.'

'It was dark,' said Tokes. 'There were loads of people, smoke everywhere. Maybe it won't be clear who did what.'

I thought again of the images on my own camera: the knife in Shiv's hand, Tokes trying to pull him away, Shiv launching himself at Ishmael.

'I filmed it too,' I muttered quietly. 'I filmed the stabbing.'

Tokes narrowed his eyes and looked at me oddly. 'Seriously?'

'I forgot I had the camera running,' I tried to explain, knowing how it sounded. 'It just all happened . . .'

Tokes frowned. 'Did you watch it?'

I nodded my head. The images were still running through my head on an endless loop, and I wondered if I'd ever stop seeing them.

'Does it show, you know, what really happened?' he asked anxiously.

I nodded again. 'It's obvious you were only trying to help. That Shiv was the one who did it.'

Tokes still looked nervous. 'Can I see it?'

'My camera got smashed,' I said. 'But the memory card is fine. And I've got it all backed up on my laptop.'

'Have you got the camera with you?'

I shook my head. 'Pea told me to throw it away,' I said, the words tumbling quickly out of me now. 'But he doesn't know about the backup.'

'So what did you do with it?' Tokes was looking at me, his brow wrinkled in anxiety. 'The camera.'

'I hid it.'

We walked in silence past the furniture shop which was now a burned-out shell, still smouldering in places. I couldn't stop staring at the blackened walls, the warped shapes, the odd recognisable item among the charred forest of stuff.

Down by Iceland somebody had started sticking Post-it notes on to the boarded-up windows where my mum had been doing her interview. They said things like *Stop destroying our homes* and *Coronation Road community united against the rioters.* They'd left a load of ballpoint pens and multicoloured Post-its so other people could put up messages too.

And there were pictures up as well – grainy stills from CCTV footage, images of hooded faces, half caught in the camera's gaze.

And standing staring up at the gallery of faces was Little Pea.

He didn't look good at all. The right side of his face was swollen and he looked even smaller than usual which is saying something. He was staring at the pictures and he seemed to be muttering to himself as his beady little eyes flicked from face to face.

He jumped to attention when he saw us, then looked around shiftily as if he was working out whether to leg it.

'Hey, peeps,' he chirruped. 'How you doin' this mornin', huh?'

'Fine,' said Tokes. 'No thanks to you.'

'Hey, no hard feelin's, blud. I cuttn't hang around. Had important business elsewhere and I could see you had da situation covered, innit.' He blinked a few times. 'That shop boy – he make it to hospital, right? I seen it on TV. He not dead or nuttin'.'

'Not yet, no,' Tokes replied. 'He still hasn't woken up.'

'That mean he not able to ID who stabbed him then,' squeaked Pea happily. 'That good news, right?'

'Is it?' asked Tokes angrily. 'For who?'

Pea kept looking around, like he was waiting for something to jump out of the shop windows and get him. 'My mamma wants me to hand myself in.' He giggled, but there was a frightened edge to his laughter. 'It's your mamma what give her da idea,' he said to me. 'She on TV goin' on about how parents should shop their own kids. My mamma was totes into that. She always think da worst of me, my old lady. No trust.'

'She was right though,' Tokes responded gruffly. 'You took stuff.'

Pea checked behind him like he was in some cop show on TV. 'Sure, everyone did, didn't they?'

'I didn't,' said Tokes.

'Yeah, well, you a freak, man!' he giggled. 'An' Hollywood did.'

He and Tokes both turned to look at me. I felt myself reddening.

Pea grinned. 'Yeah, she bag herself a sweet new camera, thanks to da Pea-man!'

'Is that true, Maggie?' I could feel Tokes staring at me.

'It's not what it sounds like,' I stammered.

'Posh girl gone over to da dark side, innit,' squeaked Pea, doing a happy little jig. 'Told you I was a bad influence, right?'

I looked up and could see Tokes's confusion. 'How could you do that?'

'Never mind that, T-man. It all gonna kick off again later, I reckon, so you get your chance to bag a few bargains if you like.'

'You're not serious,' said Tokes, turning away from me and fixing Pea with the same shocked stare.

'Am too. Reckon it gonna be bigger an' better tonight, innit,' said Pea excitedly. 'Gonna spread to neighbouring hoods – go viral, nationwide. It not even 'bout Pats no more or 'bout gettin' at da police. Peeps got a taste for it, I reckon. I'm totes up for another night of fun, me!'

'How can you even think about that after everything that's happened?' demanded Tokes, shaking his head disbelievingly. 'If you ask me, you deserve to go straight to jail if you go out looting while Ishmael Choudhary is still fighting for his life.'

Pea giggled, waving a hand theatrically at the gallery of faces. 'Hey, man, it don't count if you don't get caught. And none of us got our pictures up here.'

'Yet,' muttered Tokes, glancing quickly at me.

Pea grinned then his eyes seemed to light up as he remembered something. 'Ooh, only when Shiv find out you film him stabbin' your shopkeeper boyfrien', prison gonna be safest place for you, I reckon!'

'Keep your voice down,' Tokes hissed, glancing nervously around. Then he tugged Little Pea down the nearest alleyway, away from the little knot of people gathered round the photo gallery.

'Hey, I seed her film a felony, that all I sayin'!' protested Pea, wiggling out of Tokes's grasp and straightening his T-shirt with a proud little shimmy.

We were standing in the place we'd found Pea last night, tucked up in a ball. Now he was preening like a peacock.

'Anyway, my camera's broken,' I stammered, nervous suddenly. 'You saw – you were the one who made me drop it.'

Some instinct told me not to tell Pea I'd been able to retrieve the footage anyway, that I even had it backed up on my laptop at home. Tokes had said that secrets were currency, and I suppose I figured the less Pea knew, the better.

But it was like he could read my mind. 'Mebbe there still stuff on da memory card,' Pea said, his expression more serious suddenly.

I glanced at Tokes and he gave a tiny, barely perceptible shake of his head, like he was telling me to keep my mouth shut.

'No, there's not – honestly!' I lied. 'I – I checked.'

'Good!' said Pea. 'An' you dumped it like I said yet? Just to make sure?'

'Um – sort of.'

'Jeez, you need to get rid.' There was an edge of nervousness creeping into his voice. 'I tellin' you this as a frien'. Da sooner that camera disappear off da face of da earth, da safer you be. We all be! Tell me you gonna get rid of it, girl?'

'I – I am,' I stuttered. 'I did. I mean, it's all taken care of.'

'It better be!' said Pea, looking at me suspiciously, like he wasn't sure he believed me. 'Cos you don't wanna go gettin' no crazy-fool ideas 'bout handin' that footage to da feds, y'hear. If you do then none of our lives be worth livin' no more, you know that, right?'

I glanced at Tokes again, but this time his expression was closed, unreadable. He wouldn't even look at me properly.

And I wondered if that was what he had in mind. If he thought we should hand the footage to the police, to make sure Shiv was punished for what he did. I felt sick suddenly.

'No, no, of course not,' I said quickly.

Tokes's eyes flicked up to mine and away again as I said that, and I wondered if he'd ever look at me properly again. Like he used to.

'Good!' said Pea. 'Cos that be jus' a suicide mission, innit! You both know that, don't you?'

'Shiv stabbed Ishmael Choudhary,' Tokes said quietly, glancing in my direction as he said the name. 'You think he should just get away with it?'

'I think little folks like you an' me should keep outta things what ain't none of our business,' said Pea.

Tokes stared at him. 'So you're just planning to keep on hanging with the Starfish like nothing has happened?'

'Don't see why not!' said Pea with a shrug.

Tokes shook his head. 'I don't believe it, you know,' he said. 'This act of yours – like you don't know right from wrong.'

'Jus' ask my mamma,' Pea said defiantly. 'She tell you. I born that way.'

'Nobody's born bad,' said Tokes.

'I mus' be the exception then!'

Tokes stared at him so hard that Pea squirmed a little. 'You can pretend all you like, but you know what's right, same as anyone else,' Tokes said. 'And you can choose to do the right thing or you can choose not to. But it's your choice. Not DNA or statistics or destiny or the devil. *You* get to choose.'

'Well, I jus' choosin' to stay alive,' said Pea defiantly. And then he stared right back at Tokes and said, 'An' if you got any sense you'll do da same.'

He said that like it was a challenge and he kept looking at Tokes as he said it. And Tokes stared back and didn't look away.

Just then my phone started ringing. I tugged it out of my pocket and stared at the screen. It was my mum.

SCENE 22: THE LOUNGE IN MAGGIE'S HOUSE

'Have you seen this?'

She was sitting in the lounge, yellow marigolds on the glass coffee table, her suit jacket flung over the back of my dad's favourite leather chair. On the table in front of her were several blown-up photographs. They were fuzzy, dark, blurry. I think I knew as soon as I walked in what they were.

'Your hair is pretty distinctive, Maggie.'

I took a step forward. She was right. You could make out a mop of spiky hair, the shape of Buzz Lightyear's face on my T-shirt. You could even see some of the Tippex patterns on my boots. And Tokes too. Even with his hood up his face was clearly identifiable.

'Are you telling me that's not you?' My mum turned to look at me.

'It's not what it looks like . . .' I muttered.

'Oh God!' She ran her hand through her perfect hair.

'Oh God, Maggie. What have you done?'

She was looking at me like Tokes had last night, disappointment and panic etched across her face.

'Where did you get those pictures from?' I asked.

'The police are going through CCTV footage. One of their officers recognised you after your little escapade the other day,' she said.

'Mum, I . . .'

I wanted her to look at me. I wanted to tell her I was sorry. I wanted to ask for her help. But she was looking down at her hands, smoothing one over the other.

'Did you do this to ruin my career?' she asked quietly. 'Because you think I work too much?' She looked up then, looked me straight in the eye. I didn't answer. 'Did you take anything?'

I flushed, but shook my head. Tears were clouding my eyes and my head was pounding so hard I felt as if it would explode.

'And what on earth were you doing there? Can you explain that to me?' Her face had changed a bit. For once she looked like she didn't think she knew all the answers. Not like the woman on the TV screens who had promised punishment for every single rioter.

'Was it that boy? He talked you into it?'

'No! He didn't want anything to do with it. It was me. I persuaded *him* to go.'

'Why?' She was shaking her head, staring at me in disbelief. 'I'm trying to understand here, Maggie. Why?'

'At first, I just wanted to see,' I said again, but the words sounded empty, insufficient. 'To film stuff.'

She let out a laugh that was almost a sob. 'That bloody camera!' she said, her eyes to the ceiling. 'You think when you're filming you're not involved?' she said. 'That you're invisible?'

I didn't answer. That was what Tokes had said too.

'And you thought it would be fun to film what? Looting? Rioting?' She looked at me again. 'Your friends setting fire to buildings? A young man being stabbed?'

I didn't have an answer for that either.

She stood up. She wasn't wearing her heels and she looked much shorter in her stockinged feet. 'Look, I'm going to speak to my lawyer. Work out how we can keep you out of all this. We can talk properly later.'

'I thought you said parents should hand their kids over to the police,' I muttered.

She stopped for a second, then turned back to me. 'You stupid, stupid girl!' she said. I don't think she'd ever said anything like that before and I felt it sting – like the cut on my hand.

'Mum, I –'

'Look, whatever you think of me, I will not allow you to

ruin your life,' she said angrily. 'You will stay at home. You will not go out. You will not contact that boy or any of the other people who saw you last night. You will say nothing. Do you understand?'

She didn't wait for me to nod. It was non-negotiable.

'I need to make some phone calls,' she said, starting to turn away. 'The police are predicting more rioting tonight. I really could have done without this, Maggie.'

'Has Dad called?' I asked.

She gave another laugh that sounded more like a sob. When I looked at her then, I could see her eyes were unnaturally bright, like she was trying not to cry. But she just said, 'I'm afraid not.'

I nodded and glanced back at the photos on the coffee table. In one of them my face was looking right at the camera. It was very blurred, but I wondered if the police had those computer people who could make even the fuzziest images clean again. Maybe they could work out what was going on in my eyes because I couldn't.

'What about Tokes?' I asked.

She looked at me then like she hardly knew me. 'He stabbed Mr Choudhary's son, what do you think is going to happen to him?'

'No!' I cried, my heart leaping suddenly in my chest. 'Tokes tried to stop it. He tried to stop Shiv.'

'That's not what it looks like on the footage,' she said.

'I don't understand.' My heart was beating frantically suddenly and my gut was twisted with sickness and fear. 'How can it . . .? He was trying to help.'

'I've seen it myself,' Mum insisted calmly. 'It shows your friend pushing another teenager aside and stabbing Mr Choudhary's son with the other boy's knife.'

'But that's not what happened!' I yelled. 'It was Shiv. Tokes was trying to stop him.' I was breathless now, the words tumbling out of me, frantic to make myself understood. 'I promise you it wasn't Tokes. Let me talk to the police. I can tell them what happened. I saw everything.'

'No!' She waved a hand. 'You will say nothing at all until I have spoken to my lawyer.'

'But, Mum . . .'

'But nothing. For once, Maggie, I need you to do as you are told.' Her voice was like stone. She moved towards the door, stockinged feet soundless on the thick red carpet. I remembered what Tokes told me, about the boy in the book who met the posh girl, and the cobwebby lady who lured him like a spider to her web and tangled him in the threads. I realised with a jolt that the posh girl was me and that I still had no idea how the story ended.

'Mum,' I said desperately. 'I filmed it. I filmed what happened.'

She spun round quickly. 'You have film footage of the stabbing?'

I nodded. 'And it shows it wasn't Tokes. It proves he was innocent.'

I don't think she was even thinking about Tokes any more. 'Where is it?' she demanded.

'It's still on my camera,' I lied. At least it was only half a lie, because it was still there, unless Pea had figured out somehow that I'd stashed it, and she didn't need to know it was backed up on my laptop upstairs. I needed an excuse to get out of the house. To warn Tokes.

'And where is your camera?'

'It's . . . I hid it . . .'

She raised a perfectly manicured eyebrow. Then she said simply, 'Get the camera. I will phone my lawyer.'

'Why?'

'Because just maybe the police will agree to keep you out of it in return for footage that helps them convict whoever is responsible for the stabbing.'

She was speaking more like a politician now than a mother. I could almost see the cogs in her brain ticking away in work mode, mum mode forgotten.

'What about Tokes?' I asked again.

She looked up. 'If the film shows he did nothing as you say he did,' she said, 'then he should be fine. Shouldn't he?'

SCENE 23: BEHIND THE FISH FACTORY

I caught sight of Mr Choudhary on the TV on my way out. Petra had the news on in the kitchen and he was giving an interview. I stopped in the doorway, frozen to the spot as the lens closed in on his face.

'We must stop this madness and bring peace back to our community,' Mr Choudhary was saying. He was looking right at the TV camera as he spoke and his eyes were full of hurt. His moustache was neatly combed now and he had sorted out his tie, but he was still wearing the same rumpled shirt he'd had on earlier.

'My beloved son is lying in a critical condition in hospital,' he went on, his voice cracking on the final word. He swallowed, then regained his composure. 'He tried to defend our community and now he is badly hurt. And so too our community is hurt by what has happened.' He spoke with a quiet dignity. In the background I could see the damaged shopfront of Choudhary's Electrical Store, the police incident tape.

'So I call for a stop to this madness,' Mr Choudhary continued. 'There must be no more. No more rioting, no more looting, no more hurting.'

He stared right at the screen as he said that and I felt as if he was looking right at me. My stomach contracted again at the thought of the new camera under my bed and I couldn't watch any more. I turned and ran out of the house, pushing open the door and bursting out on to the street, gulping the hot air into my lungs. Then I ran straight to the yard. I needed to see Tokes and I was sure that's where he'd be.

As I pushed my way under the fence, it felt cooler than it had for days, and the smell of rain was in the air. Tokes was there, just like I'd thought he would be. But someone else had got there before us. The whole place had been trashed. The plant pots, the funny little sculpture – all smashed. The sofa was upturned, cushions slashed and ripped, contents strewn all over the place.

'No!' I gasped. I started rummaging around in the scattered innards of the sofa. 'No! It's gone!'

'Maggie, what's the matter?' Tokes had his hand on my arm and for a moment he sounded like the old Tokes. 'You've been crying. What happened?'

'My camera,' I said. 'Someone's taken it.'

'Pea beat us to it, I guess.'

I stared up at him and I knew straight away he was right.

'But the police – they think you stabbed Ishmael,' I stammered, looking up into his beautiful, sunshine face and watching it darken.

'What?' His eyes filled with alarm.

'The CCTV footage makes it look like you did it. Mum says they're going to arrest you.'

From the platform above a baby's cry rose into the hot summer sky. Tokes just stood there, looking down at me, and said nothing.

'We have to give them my film because that proves you're innocent.'

Still he stood there, his face ashen. Then he said quietly, 'You've got it on the laptop, right?'

'Yes, but if Pea's got the camera –' I broke off, because suddenly I knew exactly what Pea had done with it. 'Tokes, what if he gave it to Shiv?'

Tokes nodded his head slowly, like he was struggling to process everything. I watched him, waiting to see what he was going to say. He slumped down on the sofa, leaned back and stretched out his long legs. There was a stillness about him this morning, a quietness that was almost unnerving, and when he did speak all he said was, 'I spoke to my dad.'

I wasn't expecting that. But afterwards I thought it was just like what happens in the movies. That moment – right in the heat of the action, just before the final showdown – when everything slows down and the main character starts talking about the stuff that really matters. It's called the 'point of commitment' according to my movie magazine.

'There's a phone box in the station,' he was going on, his finger running along the worn fabric of the sofa. 'I called Dad on his mobile. It was weird to hear his voice.'

'Why?' I asked. It felt like I was filming him, interviewing him, even though I didn't have a camera in my hand. 'Why did you call him?'

'I thought he might know what to do.' He shrugged, then gave a funny sort of smile. 'He's not so good at helping with homework – maths and chemistry and that – but he knows a bit about this kind of thing, I reckon.'

'Right.' I glanced down at his fingers drawing patterns. 'So what did he say?'

'He said if we turn that film in to the police we're as good as dead.' He hesitated, a resigned expression on his face.

I looked at his long-legged figure on the sofa and realised how tall he was. I'm not sure I'd ever properly noticed before.

'But he still says we should hand it in,' he went on.

'Yes, because if we don't you're going to be arrested for murder.'

'I suppose,' he said thoughtfully, as if that wasn't a big deal. 'Dad says we've got to go straight. Straight as an arrow. From the beginning. For always. No matter what.' He looked up at me then, looked at me properly. 'He says once you start lying you're already caught in the web and you'll never get out.'

'And maybe it will be OK anyway,' I said, desperate suddenly for this not to be how it ended. 'Maybe Ishmael will wake up and identify Shiv and they won't even need to use the footage. Maybe a witness will come forward.'

And just then the flap opened and Little Pea wriggled through.

'Pea! What are you . . .?'

Pea's face was pale and he seemed to be shivering, like he had a fever or something.

'Hi, peeps!' he squeaked, trying to be upbeat but not quite managing his usual smile. 'So whassup?'

'You took my camera,' I said angrily. 'Again!'

'Course I did. I figure somebody had to save you from yourself.'

'What did you do with it this time?'

Tokes was staring up at the station platform above.

'I give it Shiv, dittn't I?' Pea said matter-of-factly.

I stared at him in horror.

'Look, I not an idiot,' he said. 'I guess right off what North London boy here had in mind. An' handin' it to da police – that a suicide mission,' Pea went on. 'So I give da camera to Shiv. An' –' he paused dramatically, a bright smile spreading all over his face – 'you never guess what!'

'What?' said Tokes wearily.

'I quit da Starfish!'

'What?'

'I told Shiv this is da last job I gonna do for him.' Pea's eyes were shining proudly though he was still shivering. 'Told him I want outta da gang. I'm gonna get me a new start, just like you said.'

Tokes let out a sound that was halfway between a laugh and a groan.

'But, Pea . . .' I said.

'I been thinkin' 'bout it, see,' Pea chattered on excitedly. 'Decided there ain't no reason why da Pea can't go straight. I gonna take back all da stuff I stole, work me hard at school, turn over every leaf in da book. Then mebbe I can hang wit' you?'

He looked at us hopefully. Like a dog that wants a pat.

'Pea, you don't know what you've done,' I said quietly.

'I save your skin givin' Shiv that camera!' Pea squeaked. 'I done da right thing, innit. Jus' like Mr Tokes said I should.'

'How was that the right thing to do?' demanded Tokes.

'Now Shiv leave us all alone an' we can get us all them happy endin's, innit.'

He said the last bit with a little bow, followed by a skip. I glanced at Tokes, whose face was twisted with anxiety.

'But we have to give the film to the police,' I said quietly, 'or they're going to arrest Tokes for murder. They think he did it.'

'For real?' said Pea, eyes widening in surprise.

'The CCTV makes it look like it was Tokes.'

Pea whistled through his teeth. 'Well, he still be safer in jail than if he grass on Shiv,' he declared, unmoved.

'We're handing the film in, Pea,' I said quietly.

Pea shuffled a little then said, with a nervous smile, ''Fraid it too late for that, innit. Camera custody of Mr Shiv Karunga.'

I glanced at Tokes, but neither of us said anything.

'What?' demanded Pea, looking from me to Tokes like he could tell there was something up. 'What you sayin'? You keep da memory card? You got backup somewhere? What?'

I looked down at my feet and beside me I could feel Tokes shift uncomfortably.

Pea gave a little squeak like a cartoon mouse. It would have been funny if he hadn't looked so terrified. 'You gotta be kiddin'!' he said. 'Tell me you're kiddin', right?'

Tokes just shrugged. The baby on the platform had started crying again and hiccuping sobs filled the air above us.

'No!' Pea's face had crumpled like paper and his cry joined with the baby's. 'No way, man. I don't believe you! You jus' bluffin'!'

Tokes shook his head.

Pea's eyes were dancing with fear. 'Why dittn't you say? I tell Shiv it was da only copy.' Pea shivered like he had a fever and neither Tokes nor I said anything.

'Well then –' Pea stuttered. 'You gotta give it to Shiv, you unnerstand? No choice. Cos if you give it to da police then Shiv come after you. He hunt you down. Both of you.'

I glanced at Tokes who just shrugged and said, 'Maybe that's the risk we have to take.'

'An' me.' Pea was panicked like I'd never seen him. 'He kill me. You unnerstand? For real. He kill me if he go down for this. Then you'll have my blood on your hands.' His eyes were blinking with fear.

'Why?' I said. 'It's not your fault.'

'You don' know Shiv!' Pea squealed. 'He a psycho – a serial killer waitin' to happen!'

'But he can't blame you for something we do.'

'He can! Don't you get it yet?' Pea said, his voice pleading, desperate. 'He say he hold me responsible for anyt'ing you two do. You mess up, I gotta pay. Only I ain't gonna let that happen.' He was breathing quickly now, his eyes darting round as he tugged his phone out of his pocket and started tapping away on the keys.

'Pea, what are you doing?' I said.

'I gonna let Shiv know,' he said.

'Pea, don't . . .' yelled Tokes, grabbing for the phone. Pea ducked and dived out of the way. 'There's no need!'

Pea stared at him, his finger on the send button. 'I got no choice, have I?' he said. 'An' mebbe my mamma right after all. Mebbe I got da devil in me like she says – can't do da right thing even when I try.' He looked up at me, eyes glistening.

Tokes made another grab for the phone, but Pea wriggled out of the way. 'Pea, that's not true . . .' he said. 'You don't have to do this. I'll give it to him. I'll give Shiv the laptop.'

'Too late,' he said, tapping a button. 'Sent!'

I stared at him and so did Tokes.

'You told Shiv?'

Pea nodded. He just looked like a scared little kid then. He was shaking a bit and his eyes were blinking like he was trying not to cry.

'Fine,' said Tokes, a look of resignation on his face.

'If I was you, I'd go get that laptop,' said Pea. 'An' any other copies of your little home movie you got stashed away too. Hand it all over to Shiv quick smart. Otherwise even Little Pea can't save you now.' He was already wriggling under the hole in the fence, like a rat burrowing into the ground. Just before he disappeared he turned and looked up at us both with big round eyes. 'Sorry,' he said quickly. 'I tried to do da right t'ing, but mebbe it's no good – for a kid like me. I left it too late.'

'Pea, that's not . . .'

But then he was gone.

I turned to Tokes who was still staring after him.

'What do we do now?' I asked.

I could hear the rumble of a train approaching overhead, the sound of the announcer on the platform, the screeching of the pigeons in the netting.

'I don't know,' said Tokes.

SCENE 24: THE PARK

You know that thing in films when the final scene is like a mirror image of the first? Well, it was like that. Because right at the very end we found ourselves back in the park.

The Starfish Gang was waiting for us. Sitting on the roundabout, spinning slowly like big black birds on a turntable. The rest of the park was deserted.

Pea was with them, perched right in the middle of the roundabout so that he was taller than everyone around him for once. King of the Castle.

It was only when you got up close that you could see Shiv had a gun up against his back.

'It's a stick-up!' Pea giggled as we came closer. I wish I'd been able to film that – the way he was grinning, even while he was trembling like a little bird.

'You get my message then?' said Shiv.

He was wearing his long leather coat again, but his cap was

off for once. I realised he was actually quite short – that he wore that big hat to make himself look taller. Without it, he looked shrunken, like an old man, but somehow more menacing than ever.

'We got it,' said Tokes, glancing anxiously at Pea.

'She bring the laptop?' Shiv nodded at me, his eyes narrowed.

My hand tightened round the straps of the rucksack on my back. I'd run back to the house to get it minutes after Pea had sent the text. I'd passed the Choudharys' house where the gifts were piling up against the railings.

'The police have got the whole thing on CCTV anyway,' said Tokes. 'You do know that, right?'

'Yeah, and we also hear they signed a warrant for your arrest soon as they watched it,' laughed Tad who was perched just behind Shiv, legs stretched out over the roundabout like a giant spider in a web.

Tokes glared at Little Pea. 'Is there anything you didn't tell them?'

Pea shrugged apologetically, but Tokes didn't wait for him to respond. 'Anyway, there were witnesses,' he went on. 'Lots of them who saw what really happened.'

Shiv just smiled, his milky-white eyes glistening. 'Like Little Pea here,' he said. 'He gonna make a statement. Confirm I was only tryin' to help that shop boy, innit.'

Tokes stared at Pea. 'Why would you do that?'

'Shiv is my bro,' said Pea with a wiggle of his head. 'He'd do the same for me.'

'Would he?'

Shiv's face cracked into a hard, thin smile, but he said nothing.

'An' I gonna sell my story to da tabloids,' Pea went on, his voice too high, quivering on the top notes. 'Tell 'em what I done, all da stuff I took. I be da face of da riots.'

'You reckon?' said Tokes.

'Yeah! Tabloids gonna love that, i'nt that right, Shiv?'

I could hardly even look at him. He had a gun against his back and his face was all mashed, but he was looking at Shiv like he was his big brother. It made me feel angry and sorry and hopeless all at the same time.

'Then I gonna have my new start,' Pea was saying. 'Ain't I, Shiv-man? I do this for you an' I free to go off turnin' over new leaves an' that?'

Next to Shiv, Tad and a few other members of the crew started laughing.

Tokes managed to keep his face and his voice calm. 'Why not turn yourself in too then, Shiv?'

Shiv stopped grinning and let out a low, hissing growl. 'You think you funny, North London boy?'

'Not really.'

Shiv jumped down off the roundabout, landed like a jaguar, then slid forward, dragging Pea with him until he was just a few metres in front of us.

My palm was hot and damp round the strap of my rucksack. When I had run home to get it, my mum had been in the lounge, on the phone to someone – her lawyer probably. As I tugged open the front door to leave, I could hear her shouting, 'Where do you think you're going, Maggie? Come back here this minute. Don't you dare run out on me . . . . Maggie, please . . .' I'd wanted more than anything to turn round, run to her, fling myself into her arms and ask for her help, but it was too late. There was a stolen camera under my bed and a man fighting for his life in hospital and Tokes was going to be arrested. And it was all my fault.

So now I was standing in the park with my laptop in my bag and I still didn't know what I was going to do with it. There was a deep well of panic in my belly and I felt like my legs were going to crumple under me. I didn't trust myself to do anything, let alone the right thing.

'There could be other witnesses,' Tokes was saying.

Shiv draped his hand round Little Pea. The gun was now nestling against Pea's neck like a caress. Pea was stiff as a board, his eyes round with terror, his mouth set into a weird plastic grin in his bruised face. 'Look, whatever you think you see last night you need to forget it,' Shiv hissed. 'Unless you want your little friend to get it in the neck.'

'But I've got a good memory,' Tokes said, his voice still unwavering. 'Like an elephant.'

'Yeah, well, brain damage has a way of curing that problem, innit,' said Shiv, taking another swaggering step towards us.

I think I still thought it wasn't real. It was a scene from a movie. And, even though I'd seen Shiv stick a knife into Ishmael, I didn't think he'd really hurt Pea. In broad daylight. In a kids' playground.

'Enough of the chitchat,' said Shiv. I remembered that this was the boy who they said had broken his own mum's jaw. 'You got somethin' for me? You an' your polly-tician girlfriend.'

My hand gripped the strap of my rucksack even tighter.

'We've got it,' said Tokes, glancing quickly at me.

'How I know she not made copies?'

'You've got to trust us, I s'pose,' Tokes replied.

Shiv tugged Little Pea forward like he was a dog on a lead and I saw him stumble for a second then right himself, his grin disappearing for the tiniest of seconds before reattaching itself to his battered face.

'Lucky I got me some insurance policy then, innit,' said Shiv.

'What insurance is that, Shiv-man?' said Pea with a nervous giggle.

'It's simple. If the police get hold of that footage – any time, any how –' He spoke coolly, evenly, like he was talking about the weather. His pale eyes were motionless and blank like mirrors. I could see Tokes reflected in them, staring back at him as he said, 'Then Pea bites the dust, right?'

There was a second's pause before Pea started giggling insanely. 'You kiddin', right, Shiv-man?'

Tokes glanced first at Pea then at Shiv.

'You don't mean that,' said Tokes, his voice a little less certain now.

'I dead serious,' said Shiv. 'You try to send me down and I won't just ruin your lives, I'll shoot this Pea-boy dead. Anyt'ing you don't unnerstand about that?'

The sun was shining and I could hear the sound of children's laughter from somewhere close by. I could smell barbecues, and little ice-cream clouds were scudding across the brilliant blue sky above. It didn't feel like the sort of day when this should be happening.

'Cos it's not like his mum will miss him, issit?' Shiv went on, tugging Pea closer to him so that his face was squashed right up against Shiv's chest. 'She always say you get youself shot one day, innit, Pea-man. She always say it.'

'Yeah, Shiv,' said Pea, his head twisted, grinning up at Shiv like he was having a joke. 'That what she say.'

Tokes looked at Little Pea then, and Pea stared back with a

sudden desperation in his eyes. It looked like they were having a staring contest, that Pea would stay alive so long as neither of them looked away, no one blinked.

'Well, this is the only copy of the film,' Tokes said, speaking directly to Pea, like he was making a promise. 'Once you have this, there's no way we can give it to the police, even if we want to.'

'That good news for Little Pea then, innit!' said Shiv. He was staring hard at me now, his eyes burning holes in my face. 'Now give me that laptop before my patience run out,' he said, pressing the gun hard against Pea's temple.

Pea gave a little squeak. Tokes didn't break eye contact with him as he said, 'Maggie – give me the bag.'

I thought of Tokes being charged with the stabbing, Shiv getting away with it.

'Do as your North London boyfriend says,' hissed Shiv. 'Hand over the bag an' you go back to your posh life. You get outta jail free, rich girl, innit.'

I couldn't breathe. There seemed to be no right thing any more. Whatever I did was wrong.

'You'll be arrested, Tokes,' I whispered.

But Tokes didn't move his eyes away from Little Pea's. 'Just give him the bag, Maggie.'

I willed him to look at me. 'They'll lock you away. All your plans . . . your mum wanted you to have a better life.'

'None of that matters any more,' Tokes sighed, still holding Pea's gaze, keeping his promise. 'Give him the bag,' he said again, through gritted teeth.

'Yeah, I's kind of in a bit of a situation here . . .' said Little Pea who was as still as I'd ever known him. 'I don't know if you noticed, but I gotta gun up 'gainst my head, gonna blow my brains out.'

'You worried 'bout losin' your computer, rich kid?' called out Tad. I noticed he'd shaved off one of his eyebrows and it made his face look lopsided. 'Cos we pick up lots of 'lectrical goods real cheap last night,' he said, laughing.

The rest of the Starfish Gang laughed along with him, and I thought of the hooded figures running out of Choudhary's Electrical Store, right over Ishmael, soaking wet with blood on the ground.

'Get you a new camera an' all,' said Tad. 'Kit you out jus' like before. Clean stock. No memory. Y'hear what I sayin'?'

My head was reeling now – the camera under my bed, the bag on my back, the blood on the pavement, the footage from the first time in the park. The geeky girl with a camera, standing by and doing nothing. Again.

'No,' I said. The word came out like a sob, but as soon as it was out there, in the fizzing hot air, I knew I couldn't take it back.

Shiv's eyes narrowed and his body seemed to snarl. 'What you sayin', girl?'

'Maggie, just hand it over,' said Tokes, eyes darting quickly to me and back to Pea again.

'No.' I was barely breathing now. All I could think was that I needed to step up. Do the right thing. Stand up for my friend . . . properly this time.

'Maggie . . .' Tokes was pleading.

'You wanna know what happen if you don't give me that laptop?' said Shiv.

I always thought that slow motion only happened in films. But it turns out I was wrong. Everything had slowed down to about five frames per second; even the sound was blurry.

'Maggie, please . . .' I'm not sure who said that. Tokes or Pea?

'I tell you what happen,' Shiv went on. 'First I shoot Pea, then I shoot him.' He waved the gun in Tokes's direction, then pointed it at me. 'Then I come after you. One – after – the – other.'

'No,' I said again. It was like I couldn't say anything else now. I couldn't let Tokes ruin his life. Not because of me.

'You don' believe me?' Shiv's eyes were bulging now. 'I give you a little proof then . . . youngest first.'

I didn't believe he'd do it.

‘No!’ It was Tokes who was shouting out now. And running forward, screaming – loud, clear vowels rising up towards the clouds.

Pea was screaming too. ‘No! Shiv-man! Please, man! No! What ’bout my new start, man!’

Tokes reached him and for a second I thought it was going to be like the first time – that he was going to save the day.

Then a shot rang out. Loud and clear across the park. Little Pea’s face registered surprise at first. His feet twitched, arms too, like he was moonwalking or the devil in his veins was dancing its way out of him. He let out a little cry. And then he slumped to the ground.

SCENE 25: THE PARK. MOMENTS LATER

I didn't have a camera to film what happened afterwards, but, when I remember it, it's like I'm watching a movie. This is how the movie ends.

The camera starts off high above the scene, looking down on it from way, way above. You can see a park. It's empty, apart from two teenagers and a kid who is lying on the concrete, a stain of red gradually spreading out from his body. From this height all three figures look minuscule. Like dolls or puppets. You can't hear what they're saying – their voices are tiny against the roar of traffic, the wail of distant sirens, children laughing somewhere nearby.

Then the camera pans slowly round so you can see all that lies beyond the park: the huge high-rise housing estate to the south and west; the rows of terraces to the east; and the distinct skyline of the city to the north, glinting in the sunlight reflected off the River Thames.

As the camera rotates, it takes in the vastness of the city. Then it moves slowly downwards, closer to the three figures so that we start to be able to see them a bit better. One has purple hair that looks like she cut it herself. She is dressed like a skinny street urchin and she wears a pair of cherry-red boots with faces Tippexed on the toes. The other has skin the colour of chocolate, eyes like pebbles and a cloud of brown hair.

He's cradling the third – a younger boy, so small he looks like a rag doll with a pea-shaped face and scars all over his head. The older boy's hands are pressed to the boy's chest and they are covered in blood. The girl kneels to the other side of the bleeding boy. She has blood on her hands too.

The camera comes in closer, rotates again so that you can see the scene close up from every angle. The bleeding boy is wearing brand-new designer trainers that look far too big for him. The girl is crying and fumbling in her pocket.

'Tokes, we should call somebody,' she is saying. Her voice is trembling like a leaf on a tree; her face is colourless, blank.

'Call an ambulance,' the older boy – Tokes – is saying.

The girl makes a call, but you can tell they both know it's no use. The camera knows this too. 'Ambulance. Starfish Park, Coronation Road. A boy's been shot,' she says, knowing already they'll never make it on time.

The bleeding boy opens his eyes for the first time. They are two bright pinpricks in his small round face. He mutters something that the camera cannot pick up.

'What's that?' Tokes leans in to listen. The camera does too.

The girl puts her hand to her mouth. For a second, just for a second – you can see it in her eyes – she thinks everything is going to be OK. He's awake and talking.

The boy with the pea-shaped face gives a little splutter then manages to get some words out. The camera is trained tightly on his face now to pick up every syllable. 'Tell my mamma,' he whispers, his eyes twinkling, dancing like his feet that had never seemed to be still.

'You want us to call her?' says Tokes, his voice off-camera.

'No.' The boy manages a tiny smile. 'Jus' tell her . . .' He gasps, a slow, rattling breath, then swallows and says, 'Tell her . . . I was . . . a good boy.'

'What?' says Tokes. The camera cross-fades to his face now. His eyes are full of tears.

'Tell her . . . I done nuttin' wrong,' the boy whispers, so quiet the camera barely picks it up. 'She will think it all my fault . . . That I brung it all on myself.' He heaves another long breath which seems to wrack his whole body. 'But you gotta tell her . . . I was a good boy. I turn good in da end.'

'We will,' says Tokes. His voice is choked.

'*You* tell her.' The boy is saying this to the girl now. His eyes are locked on hers and they seem to fill the whole screen.

'She believe it if you say it. Nice white girl like you. She believe I made a new start if you tell her.'

The girl is crying now. She is no use to anyone any more. She knows this is all her fault. And it was all for nothing because her rucksack is gone, wrenched from her hands after the gunshot. She is crying and her bloody hands are in her hair and on her face, staining them both the colour of her boots.

'Promise,' says Little Pea, the word barely more than a sigh.

'I promise,' she whispers.

He gives a faint smile, then he gulps and his body twitches and shudders.

The camera twists away then, spiralling up into the sky to take in the panorama of the city. It circles ever higher, so that everything below looks smaller and smaller. And, as it rises, a small boy dies below. Dies in the arms of a hero. While a violet-haired girl cries at his side.

SCENE 26: THE PARK, A FEW MINUTES LATER

It took several minutes for the blood to stop. Finally, I whispered, 'Is he dead?'

Tokes gave the briefest of nods. 'You should go.'

I stared around at the empty swings, where Little Pea perched in the opening scene; at the roundabout where I sat and filmed that day and where Shiv and the Starfish boys had sat waiting for us only minutes ago now.

'No,' I said.

Tiny spots of rain had started to fall, fizzing on the hot concrete and making the stifling air heavy with the smell of damp.

'The ambulance will be here any minute,' Tokes said, his hands still pressed to Pea's chest. 'Then the police right behind them.'

As if on cue, we heard the sound of the sirens again, much closer now, probably only streets away.

'I'm not going.'

Tokes looked up at me. 'You have to get out of here, Maggie.'

'No,' I said. 'Someone needs to tell the police. This is my fault.' My breath was coming in swelling sobs. 'I'm staying. I'm going to tell them everything.'

Tokes was looking right at me, calm as the sea in the face of my panic.

'The police already think you stabbed Ishmael,' I said. My words seemed to fly up into the air like bubbles bursting in panic all around me. 'If they find you here –'

'I don't care about that, Maggie.'

'And, if you turn witness, Shiv'll come after you. You heard him. He'll kill you.'

'They've got witness-protection programmes,' Tokes said, his voice quiet but insistent, pushing me away.

'So I can stay. I can tell the police. They can put me in witness protection if they want.'

'Yeah, and how are they gonna make your family disappear?' Tokes said gently. 'Your mum's face is in the news every day.'

He had a point, but I didn't want to listen to him. There was rain on my face and blood on my boots, on my hands, in my hair.

'Shiv can't get away with this,' I said. I was shivering now, hot and cold at the same time.

'He won't. I won't let him.'

I stared at him. He stared at me. And somewhere, deep below my pounding heart and the waves of panic, I wanted to kiss him, full on the lips, to feel his face pressed against mine, to feel the life pounding in his chest, the blood in our veins, alive, warm.

I could hear the sirens only a street or so away and I knew I should run before they came. But I stared down at Little Pea, still lying in Tokes's arms. He looked like a child, fast asleep. He was always getting us into some kind of trouble, and half the words that came out of his mouth were a lie, but in the end no one was looking out for him. No one was there for him. Apart from Tokes.

'No,' I muttered, looking right into Tokes's beautiful eyes, knowing I'd never kiss him now, because something was spoiled forever. 'It's like your dad said,' I managed to say. 'You've got to do the right thing no matter what. Otherwise you get caught in the web.'

'Maggie . . .'

The ambulance was visible at the bottom of the park. The paramedics were climbing out of it and running towards us.

'I've done the wrong thing too long,' I said simply, tears falling as fast as the rain. 'And you said we should stick together. So I'm not leaving you. Not this time.'

SCENE 27: A HOUSE BY THE SEA. ONE YEAR LATER

The shooting of Little Pea brought the riots to an end. That and the rain that came in torrents all that day and the next, washing the blood from the park and Coronation Road. And after the rain came an army of tidy-up volunteers, armed with brushes and bin bags. Good neighbourliness fighting back against the bad.

It helped that the police announced there was going to be an inquiry into the arrest of Pats Karunga. That took the fight out of the rioters, just like Tokes had said it would, because they didn't have a cause any more.

And Mr Choudhary's call for peace changed the mood too, especially when Ishmael was pronounced out of danger.

But, most of all, the death of Little Pea shocked the nation. He was on the front of every paper, every news report. He became the 'face of the riots', just as he'd predicted. I think he'd actually have enjoyed all the fuss and attention: his fifteen minutes of fame.

My mum resigned. It was a big scandal, after the CCTV images of me on the night of the riots was leaked: 'MP girl in riot rap!' . . . 'MP mum shops her riot kid'. Stuff like that. Not that most of what the media said was even true. They really went for her at first, saying it was the end of her career, and one newspaper even called her the most hated woman in Britain.

But they were wrong, as it happened. After the fuss died down, she started getting asked to do TV and magazine interviews. They asked her about 'juggling motherhood and politics', 'parenting a troubled teen' and 'coming to terms with failing as a parent'. It made her seem more human apparently. Just a regular mum struggling with the same issues other families have. Her approval ratings shot up until they were higher than they'd ever been.

She's had loads of job offers too. Everything from charity ambassador to appearing on *I'm a Celebrity*. She was even asked to stand for the party in a local by-election. She refused them all though. As she told the readers of *Woman and Home* magazine, she was taking time out from politics 'to reconnect with her daughter', because her experiences had taught her that 'family must always come first'.

It means she's around more, and she's trying, but it doesn't mean she's become a perfect mum overnight. I always thought I wanted her to be the kind of mum who made cupcakes and helped me with my homework and chatted to me about clothes and boys and how my day at school went. Turns out neither of us is much good at that stuff.

It changed things with me and my dad too. He blamed Mum for everything that happened. He said she should have let me face the consequences of my actions, should have let me make a statement to the police, testify in the Little Pea trial, go into witness protection if necessary. He said that what she did wasn't to protect me, but to protect her career.

But she told him he wasn't around enough to be entitled to an opinion. She called him a phantom parent, a doughnut dad. She even told him I'm sick of Krispy Kremes. I heard her yelling down the phone at him and part of me wanted to laugh or cheer. The other part of me hoped he'd make more of an effort to see me. But he just stopped sending doughnuts and started sending clothes and perfume and make-up instead. He even sent me a new camera. HD, high spec – the best on the market. He keeps saying that I should come over to New York and stay with him and his new girlfriend, but it never seems to happen. And I'm not sure I care any more.

So now we live by the sea, my mum and me. She drives me to school every day and picks me up too. No more au pairs, just expensive, useless therapy sessions. Everything has changed, but nothing has changed. And I have nightmares every single night.

Mum and I are sitting eating breakfast together. We do this most days now. Neither of us says much.

It's nearing the end of the holidays. The weather is turning. School starts again soon and then Mum has to go to London to testify in the Pats Karunga inquiry. Outside it feels like the summer is already dying.

'Do you feel OK about going back?' Mum asks.

I shrug. 'I guess.'

'Are you going to join the Film Club this year?'

'Maybe,' I say.

She glances down at her coffee. Recently, people have started to say she looks like me. Or I look like her – I guess it must be that way round. Today she just looks tired and her eyes – are my eyes like that? – are pale green pools.

'Did you ever finish the film you were working on?' she asks. The question comes out of the blue – passed off as a casual enquiry – but when I look up at her face I know it's not.

I look down at my half-finished bowl of porridge. 'I'm not sure . . .' I hesitate. 'It's not really finished. I'm not sure how it ends.'

It's a funny thing to say, I suppose. Because the police

retrieved my laptop and when I got it back all the footage was still on there. So I know the ending, don't I? The film always ends the same way. Little Pea always dies. I get whisked away to the seaside. Tokes stays behind to testify in the trial that sends Shiv down. I don't. He throws away his life to do what's right, while I get to carry on as if nothing ever happened.

She stares down at her coffee and I stir the porridge with my spoon and there's only the sound of the ticking clock for a minute. And then she says, 'I watched it, Maggie.'

My head shoots up. 'What?'

'Your film. I watched it.'

I'm speechless for a second and then the anger explodes out of me. 'You had no right to do that. How did you . . .?'

'I know I shouldn't have, but I found it on your computer and I wanted to try and understand.'

My face is aflame. 'It was private,' I stammer. 'Like a diary.'

'You wouldn't talk to me,' she says quietly. 'You wouldn't talk to the counsellor.'

I look away, out of the window, over in the direction of the sea. 'I wanted to talk to the police,' I mutter. 'But you wouldn't let me.'

She sighs then, her breath like the sea breeze. 'Maggie, I'm not going to apologise for trying to protect you.'

'You said parents should make their kids hand themselves in,' I say, still staring out, unable to look at her. 'Make them take responsibility for their actions. But I told you about taking the camera and you covered up for me. I wanted to tell the police about that, and about Pea, but you wouldn't let me.'

She sighs again. 'Maggie, you may not understand or respect what I did, but I did it to protect your future. You'd have had a criminal record.'

'But I'd have done the right thing,' I say, my eyes flicking back to look at her quickly. I want to explain how the guilt sometimes feels like a solid block in my stomach, how it makes breathing hard sometimes, and words impossible.

'Sometimes people do the wrong thing for the right reasons,' she says, her eyes damp. I wonder if that's what she'll say at the inquiry too. If anyone will ever know the real truth about what happened to set this whole story in motion.

'That's not good enough.' Then I look down at my hands. Sometimes it's like I can still see Pea's blood splattered all over my white skin. 'I wanted to testify against Shiv,' I say quietly.

'I know.' She pauses. 'And I'm sorry. Maybe that was wrong of me.'

'It was.'

'And watching your film without asking your permission was wrong. There are a lot of things I haven't got right, but . . .'

'But what?'

She is looking at me, hard. She seems much older than she did a year ago. Her hair is sea-blown, coarsened by the salt air and the breezes off the ocean. And her eyes are shining with tears. My mum who never cries.

'Your film is beautiful, Maggie,' she says with a faint smile. For a second I remember the way Tokes's mum looked at him: sad but proud at the same time. That's how my mum looks now.

She hesitates. 'You're a great film-maker. And I felt very proud of you as I watched it. And I know that your friend would love it.'

'Well, he'll never see it now, will he?' I say, looking away again before my own eyes betray me. 'Besides, it's not finished.'

I watch the waves through the window. Sometimes I imagine disappearing beneath them, like they're giant teardrops swallowing me up.

'I may have an idea to help,' she says.

I look up. She's staring at me and I can't meet her eye.

'I did something I probably shouldn't have,' she says. Then she smiles wryly. 'No, I certainly shouldn't have, but I did it for you.'

'Another wrong thing for the right reasons?' I mutter.

'Perhaps, yes, probably – I don't know.' She runs a hand through her hair and I notice there are touches of grey in it now. 'I thought maybe if you could finish the film it would help. You'd –' she hesitates – 'you'd start to feel better.'

I shrug. A year has passed and I've stopped thinking I'll

ever feel better. I don't deserve to anyway.

'There's someone here to see you,' she says after a pause.

I look up. Surprised. We've hardly had a single visitor all summer.

'Who?' I ask.

'He's down on the beach,' she says.

My heart flips in my stomach and the stone of guilt dislodges slightly for a second with a flicker of hope.

'He can't stay long,' Mum goes on, and I'm staring at her, willing her to say his name, although I realise with a jolt that I don't even know what it is any more.

'And no one can know he's here or that you've seen him. You understand that?'

I nod and jump up, my heart racing so fast I can feel it in every vein in my body. Then I hesitate, look at her for a second. 'How . . .?'

'I pulled a few strings,' she says with a small smile. 'Apparently, my career is over anyway so I figured, what's a little bit more trouble?'

I stand there, caught like a reed in the wind, emotion trembling through me like a current. For a moment I can't seem to move in either direction. Then I cross the room and hug her quickly. Fiercely. No words come out.

She holds me for a second longer than I hold her. 'Go on,' she says. 'You won't have long.'

I pull away. She's looking at me. Her eyes are full of tears, but she smiles and I try to smile back. I try really hard and I almost succeed.

Then I pick up my rucksack and run out of the door, down the garden, through the tangle of forest at the bottom to the path leading to the beach.

And there he is.

SCENE 28: THE BEACH

I stop on the rocks. He's facing the sea, with his back to me, and he's skimming pebbles.

He's grown taller. His shoulders are broader and for a second I almost want to turn back. I wasn't supposed to see him again. Ever. That was the deal.

But then he turns and we stand for a moment staring at each other. I know I've changed too. My hair is mousey brown now and hangs almost to my shoulders in a regular, any-girl style. And I'm wearing one of my dad's old shirts with a pair of leggings which don't disguise how skinny I've become.

'Hi, Maggie,' he says.

'Hi,' I say, because I don't know what to call him any more.

'You look different,' he says. 'Your hair . . .'

'You too.'

I stay up on the rocks. He comes towards me and I can see

he has a soft down of hair on his chin and his face is longer than it was.

'How are you?' I ask. Then I feel myself go pink. I know the rules of witness protection. They've been explained to me often enough. 'I mean, I know you can't tell me anything, but . . .'

His face breaks into a grin and suddenly it's like the sun comes out and dances on the waves. 'No, it's OK. I'm good. New home, new school, new life. It's all good.'

'Everything worked out then? Like they promised?'

He nods. 'Yeah. It did.'

'And you're safe – you and your mum?'

He smiles gently and that makes him look like a boy again. 'And my dad too.'

'What?'

'Yeah. The witness-protection people figured if they were gonna hide us they had to make the whole family disappear.' He grins again. 'My dad's a new man – literally!'

'That's . . . amazing, right?'

'Right! He got himself a job and everything,' he says. 'Not exactly a brain surgeon, but he's doing OK. He got his second chance.'

He clambers up on to the rocks and sits down on one close to me. 'You wanna sit?'

I perch on the rock next to his, feeling shy again in front of this tall almost-stranger who used to be my friend Tokes.

'And you?' I ask, looking down at my feet, skinny and pale in battered flip-flops. 'Is it a new start for you too?'

He nods.

'You're staying out of trouble, getting top marks in school, reading lots of long books?'

He shrugs. 'You know me.'

'Friends?'

'Yeah,' he says. 'Not the same as the ones I lost, but, you know – different.'

My stomach does a weird flip and for some silly reason I want to fling my arms round his neck and cry – for Little Pea, for lost friends, for last summer and all it cost us.

I don't though.

'Hey, what about you?' he says. 'I see your mum on TV all the time.'

I roll my eyes. 'Yeah. My daughter the rioter – best thing that ever happened to her.' I bite my lip and try to grin.

He laughs. 'I'm guessing you're still not the best of friends then?'

'Not exactly, but you know –' I pause, think of the moment in the kitchen earlier. 'We're trying.'

I look down at my toes and it's like neither of us can think of anything to say for a moment. A seagull flies squawking and wheeling above. 'Remember the pigeons?'

'Poo rain,' he laughs.

'Seagulls are worse, I reckon!' I say. Then, 'Why did you come?'

'Your mum called. I don't know how.' He looks down at his hands, which are way bigger than I remember them. 'She said you were finding things hard.'

I pick at the loose skin around my chewed fingernails and don't say anything.

'She figured we needed to see each other. One last time, you know? Cos we never really got to say goodbye.' He pauses. 'My mum wasn't so sure at first, but she agreed in the end.'

'She probably thinks I ruined your life.'

'No way, Maggie!' He turns to me quickly, looks me right in the eye. 'That's not what you think, is it?'

I shrug and look away. 'That's just how it is.'

'Well, you sure tried your best to ruin it.' He starts to grin as he says it. 'But things are good for us now. Best it's ever been. Maybe you can blame yourself for that too!'

'I'm glad,' I say. 'You deserve your happy ending. You helped send Shiv down. My mum wouldn't even let me talk to the police. She – I don't know – she cut some kind of deal.'

'She did the right thing,' he says simply. 'It didn't need both of us, especially once they found the gun covered with Shiv's fingerprints. And there was no way the police could have kept you and your family safe if you'd testified.' He is looking at me like none of this is my fault and I can't bear it.

'But I didn't even tell them you were innocent.'

'Cos you didn't need to, Maggie,' he insists. 'After Ishmael Choudhary woke up, I was in the clear. No need for your film. No need for you even to be involved.'

I remembered the pictures of Ishmael on the news, his beautiful face battered almost beyond recognition. And Mr Choudhary telling a press conference outside the hospital that his beloved son was making a good recovery. That he was grateful for the people who had helped rebuild his shop – reminders of all the good in the community as well as the bad.

I also remembered Mr Choudhary's face when I'd appeared in his trashed shop with the stolen camera. My mum had told me not to go, but I knew I had to. He stood there with a dustpan and brush in his hand and he accepted my apology. He never reported me to the police, but I almost wish he had.

Tokes is looking at me.

'I left you,' I say, my stomach tightening again as I remember. 'The night of the riot. While Ishmael was bleeding. I took a stolen camera and I ran.'

Tokes hesitates for a moment then says, 'Everyone deserves a second chance, Maggie. Isn't that what we said?' I glance up at his eyes and I can see that some of the shadows from last summer are still there. 'Doing the right thing doesn't mean you never mess up. It just means you try to do better next time.'

I hold his gaze for a second and then I have to look away.

'And Ishmael is fine now,' he goes on. 'I'm fine.'

I think of Ishmael. I saw him on TV recently, playing in a charity cricket match with lots of celebrities. They were raising money for inner-city youth projects and he was standing next to Andrew Flintoff and Michael Vaughan, grinning happily, although I noticed that his hair was thinner on top and he looked older somehow.

He looked at the camera and talked about communities working together, and the need to give hope to kids who felt society had given up on them. His eyes seemed to look straight at me through the lens, but my stomach didn't flip like it used to. I glance up and realise Tokes is watching me, waiting for me to say something.

'You sound different,' I say quietly. I can't explain how, but he does. His accent is different, or maybe he just sounds older. I can't quite put my finger on it.

He leans back on the rock and keeps looking up at me. I can feel him staring even though I keep my eyes on the sea.

'I keep thinking about it,' he says. 'Can't stop seeing things. Is it the same for you?'

I nod, but still don't turn round. The sea breeze brings the smell of salt into my nostrils and my eyes hurt with uncried tears again.

'I keep thinking about our film too. Wondering if you'd finished it. Have you?'

'Nearly,' I say. 'Not quite. I sort of changed it though.'

He sits up straight again. We're close now, only a few centimetres between us. 'Can I see it?' he asks.

I pull my laptop out of my rucksack, rest it on my knees and flip it open. Then we sit and watch it together as the tide rises higher on the pebbles, pulling away each time with a rattle and a sigh.

I've changed it quite a bit since last summer. It's not a film about urban poverty or inner-city kids running riot any more. It's not even about parallel universes. It's just a film about me and Tokes and Little Pea. About Tokes saving Pea in the park and Pea landing us in a load of trouble, telling us his secrets and his lies. About us making a film and messing around and being friends and looking out for each other and letting each other down.

There's the montage of us in the art gallery, pulling silly faces; there's Little Pea doing his Riverdance and his break-dancing. There's his face when he was beaten up, him talking about his mum, his eyes wide with fear in the yard and glistening with excitement as he hung over the fence.

There's no footage of the last time in the park, of course, or of the stabbing. I thought I'd lost the stuff from the night of the riots because I figured the police would have erased it, but when I got my laptop back it was all still on there.

So there was Pea curled in a ball behind Iceland, Pea skipping with excitement, talking about sticking it to the feds, and Pea dancing on the streets as they burned all around him.

I also found a news clip of Pea's mum being interviewed after it all happened. For some reason I expected her to be a huge woman, with wobbling double chins and several tyres round her rocking waist. But she's actually small and skinny like Pea, with a round head, same as his. I watch her face and try to work out if everything Pea said about her was true or just another one of his stories.

She doesn't cry in the interview. She looks defiantly at the camera and she says, 'He was a good boy, my Paris. A good, good boy. He mek his mamma proud even to his dying day.'

Tokes stiffens when we watch that bit, like he's finding it hard to breathe.

'Bad boys lead my Paris from the path of virtue, but he say to dem "No" and that's why they shot him. He was a good boy. A good boy, my Paris.'

Then the film flicks to an image of Pea hanging over the corrugated-iron fence, just his head and hand visible, grinning into the camera, saying, 'Hello, peeps!'

Then the film ends. Nothing more.

'That's it,' I say.

Tokes turns to me and grins. His eyes are bright. 'You did it,' he says. 'I knew you would.'

'Did what?'

He looks down at the still of Pea's face on the screen, grinning, always grinning. 'You saved Little Pea.'

I shake my head. 'He's dead because of me.'

'He's dead because of a whole load of things,' says Tokes quietly. 'Everyone let him down.'

'You didn't,' I say. 'You tried to help him. And if it wasn't for me he might still be alive.'

'Because you were trying to help *me*,' Tokes says. 'You were trying to save *my* life.'

I look up and see Tokes's face crumpled into a frown.

'You can't keep thinking like this, Maggie,' he says softly. 'It'll eat you up.'

I think of the rock in my stomach which seems to grow bigger every day.

'And look, you made something out of his rubbish life,' Tokes goes on. 'You saved a bit of Little Pea. The best bit.'

I look down at my feet, at the bits of sand between my toes, the seal-grey rock and the pebbles leading down to the tideline.

'I'm telling you,' says Tokes, 'people will watch it and then they'll know him. Know he wasn't just some kid who got stabbed and went rioting. They'll see that he was crazy and clever and twisted and funny and kind and a total liar and all that stuff. Basically, that he was a real kid, not some criminal statistic.'

'But I can't put it out there. I missed the competition deadline.'

'You can put it on YouTube. I bet people would watch it,' he says. 'And maybe it would help. Cos there are other kids like Pea. Loads of them. And maybe they can be saved, even if he can't.'

I shrug. 'I dunno. My mum . . .'

He cuts me off. 'Your mum's out there talking about all this stuff on the TV all the time. And, no offence to her, but what does she know?'

'I dunno.' I shrug.

'She wouldn't let you testify in court, but she can't stop you doing this,' says Tokes.

I look up at him and I remember the endless arguments with my mum before the court case. The screaming and rowing until I gave up trying to make her hear me.

'Anyway, I can't put it on YouTube,' I say. 'You could be recognised.'

'Then cut out the bits with me in, or blur my face or something,' Tokes insists. 'That's easy enough to do.'

'And it's not finished,' I say. 'I can't think how to end it properly.'

Tokes looks down at his hands. He's been bouncing a pebble

from one to another. 'I've got an idea,' he says with a faraway smile that I recognise from the boy I knew a year ago.

The tide has started to go out, revealing clean white sand beneath the line of pebbles. We pick out only the tiny round ones, shaped like little peas. It takes a long time. Tokes can't believe how many different colours there are. He puts some in his pockets to keep.

We lay all the pebbles we've chosen in a pile then Tokes uses a stick to etch the outline of the letters in the sand. It takes him a couple of times to get it right. Then we go round putting the pebbles in the outlines – which isn't as easy as it sounds because Tokes doesn't want our footprints all over it, so we have to rub them out as we go along.

Eventually, we're finished. We clamber back up on to the rocks to view our handiwork. The tide is nearly at its lowest point so the sand is laid out like a vast blank canvas. I imagine filming it, pulling focus back out over the beach to gradually reveal the giant letters written on the sand. 'Keep dancing, Little Pea!' they say. At the end there's a smiley pea face.

I get my new camera out of my rucksack, the one my dad got me. I carry it around with me everywhere, but I haven't used it more than a couple of times.

I flick it on and focus on the letters, running the lens over the pebble words, one by one.

After I film the writing, I turn the camera back so it's looking at me and Tokes is out of shot. He can't say anything either so he holds my gaze and mouths along silently as I say for both of us, 'Goodbye, Little Pea.'

Tokes has to go soon after that. He can't even come up to the house. 'I'm undercover, y'know,' he says with a grin.

'Pea would have liked that,' I smile. 'Secret identities . . . strictly need-to-know.'

'He'd never have been able to keep it secret though, would he?' says Tokes. 'He'd have blown my cover within five minutes, that one!'

'Yeah. Pea would have been the worst witness-protection candidate ever!' We both laugh then because it's true and I feel the stone in my stomach dislodge a little bit more.

'I'll watch out for your film,' Tokes says. 'This one – and all the others you're gonna make in the future. Bet I'll be queuing up at the box office to get into your first blockbuster one day.'

I can feel my eyes starting to fill with tears because I know that what he's really saying is goodbye. The words are different, but the meaning is the same. Words are like that.

'Maybe you'll be writing screenplays,' I say, my face tight and my voice cracked. 'We might end up working together again.'

'Maybe.' He shrugs. 'My mum reckons I need to be a doctor or a lawyer or something. She says they're more reliable jobs.'

'So I'll bump into you in hospital one day,' I say quickly, refusing to believe that this is it forever. 'You'll be treating me for an ingrowing toenail.'

'Or a case of pigeon-poo poisoning!' He laughs.

'And you'll say, "Don't I recognise you?" and I'll say, "Probably because I'm an uber-famous Hollywood film director, dontcha know!"' The words come out in a tumble, more words than I've spoken for days.

He smiles. 'And I'll say, "No, I knew you once. When you had purple hair and boxes full of Krispy Kreme doughnuts."' He hesitates. 'I miss the hair by the way.'

'I was thinking of dyeing it green,' I said.

'Like a pea!'

'Yeah, I guess. My mum will go mental.' I look down at my feet again. His are next to mine – hugely long now. Like the feet of a grown man.

'Cool, that's how I'll think of you then. With crazy coloured hair and a camera stuffed in your pocket. Then I'll recognise you when you land up in my hospital some day.'

I can feel the tears rising again, but I try to push them away. 'How will I recognise you?' I say.

I look up into his face and he looks down at me. I remember that moment on the wheelie bin, when his eyes flickered to my lips and I thought he was going to kiss me.

I wonder if he's remembering it too because he glances at my mouth then back up at my eyes. There is a moment. Just a beat. Then he smiles and says, 'We'll each take a pebble.'

He reaches down and picks up two pebbles from the beach, both perfectly round and smooth – one white, one brown, the colour of his eyes. Then he pulls a pen out of his pocket and draws a smiley face on each of them. Two pebbles, round and grinning in his palm.

He hands the brown one to me and keeps the other for himself.

'We keep them, always,' he says, his eyes serious now, not leaving mine. 'That way, when we bump into each other again, even if we're old and your green hair has gone grey, we'll know.' He reaches out and takes hold of my hand, his warm fingers tangling with my thin ones, just like they used to. 'We'll know it's still us. Maggie and Tokes.'

'And our pea pebbles.'

'Yup,' he says. 'You, me and our little peas.'

FADE TO: BLACK

THE END

Acknowledgements

This book was inspired by my 'naughty but nice' Year 10s at King Edward's School, Bath, and particularly by discussions about *Lord of the Flies* a few weeks after the 2012 London riots. Yes, that's you lot, Class of 2013 (you weren't expecting that, now were you!).

But it was also heavily influenced by the young people I worked with whilst living in Peckham and helping on outreach projects run by All Saints' Church. I am also indebted to the kids I met at the Daily Bread Street Children Project in Port Elizabeth, South Africa, as well as all those I encountered whilst working at the Siyavuka Shelter and at the All Saints Educational Development Trust in King William's Town and teaching in the surrounding schools in the former Ciskei homeland. Not forgetting, of course, the children of Otjikondo School in Namibia, who continue to be an inspiration.

I am forever grateful to the wonderfully talented members of KES Creative Writing Society – especially founding members Jeni Meadow, Amber Rollinson and James Darnton. You are all an inspiration. Not to mention 7J (2012–13), 7L (2011–2013) and 7M (2013–14), as well as my rather brilliant new Year 10s (Class of 2015!). You all make me think, make me giggle and make me want to write better – both for you and because most of you write better than me already and I need to work hard to keep up!

Thank you to all the lovely ladies of the Remarkable Freshford Mothers' Reading Society, the amazing Bath Children's Authors' Support Group and Gossip Society, the English department at KES and, of course, the Freshford playground gang – what would I do without you?

Special thanks to super brother-in-law, James Smith, for putting up with my endless technical queries, along with Thomas Thurman, Kit Watson, Claire Speed Donlan and my whole Facebook technological advice team. If I've made any mistakes in the technical elements of the plot then it will be my fault and not theirs!

To grandparents who make the juggling possible and regularly save my sanity.

To Tokes Sawyerr, because you let me steal your name and turn you into a hero!

To Zeynep Kayacan and all the other amazing teachers out there who change kids' lives by caring enough never to give up.

To Tom Hartley for a cover design so beautiful it made me cry. To Caroline Montgomery, surely the loveliest, kindest, most multi-talented agent ever; and Ali Dougal, who takes the chaos of my stories and turns them into books that are better than I believed I was capable of writing. And who never gives up on me.

And to all my Peckham people. Not just those to whom the book is dedicated but to all of you: the Albany post-natal group and the All Saints old folks' bingo gang; the Muhammed family with your honey cake, the residents of the Elm Grove crack-house and the gentlemen who lived in Holly Grove shrubbery; the church mummies, the kids on the skateboards in the park, the grumpy Rye Lane shop assistants, the passengers of the 36 bus – and everyone else. This book is for you.

And always, always thank you Joe, Elsie and Jonny. Because love is all you need.

MORE FROM CATHERINE BRUTON

My dad was killed in the 9/11 attacks in New York. The stuff in this book isn't about that, but none of it would have happened if it hadn't been for that day...

'REMARKABLE, WITTY, WISE AND COMPELLING.'
SUNDAY TIMES

Our back story was a sure-fire golden ticket to stratospheric stardom. At least, that was the plan...

'POP! IS BILLY ELLIOT MEETS THE X FACTOR VIA SHAMELESS.'
THE BOOKSELLER